L.A. McBride

GATHERING THE DEAD

A KALI JAMES NOVEL: BOOK FOUR

For Maverick, who stole my heart and made me into one of those crazy dog moms I used to make fun of.

NEWSLETTER SIGNUP

Subscribe to my newsletter for updates, announcements, contests, and bonus content: lamcbride.com/newsletter/

CHAPTER 1

$\mathcal{A}$fter three weeks of sleep deprivation, intense conditioning, and fight simulations at the Compound, standing among bolts of colorful fabric and sewing supplies felt like coming home. Part of my arrangement with Aleksei included weekly trips into Bucharest to stock up on costume-making supplies so I could sew in my downtime—not that I had an abundance of downtime. Although there were bigger sewing stores in Bucharest, this one had become my go-to because it reminded me of the Stitch Witch back in Kansas City.

"Are you finding what you need, Kali?" Claudia, the middle-aged shopkeeper, greeted me with a warm smile as she finished straightening rows of fabric. Her smile dimmed as soon as she noticed the bruise across my left cheekbone.

These days, bruises were often my only accessories. One perk of being bonded with a demon was super-fast healing, so at least they didn't stick around for long. This particular bruise was fresh from this morning's sparring match with Liv.

Seeing Claudia's concern, I wished I would have had the fore-sight to cover it with makeup.

Claudia's normally friendly face turned angry as she took in my latest injury. She stepped close to me and gripped my chin with her cool fingers, tipping my head to the side. She scowled at the bruise before capturing my gaze. "No man is worth this. You need to leave him."

She may only have been five feet tall in her sturdy heels, but Claudia was the kind of woman who would take a frying pan to the head of any man who raised a hand to a woman.

I set the bolt of pale peach satin aside with a sigh. "It's not like that." From the skeptical look she gave me, she didn't believe me. My fingers brushed against my tender cheek. "I got this from sparring practice."

She gently tapped my cheek with the pad of her finger. "You got this play fighting?"

I held her gaze. "I did."

Claudia took in my outfit, from the chic houndstooth cigarette pants to the blousy peasant top. Since I only got the chance to wear something other than the standard Compound-issued black tank top and athletic pants once a week, I wasn't about to waste the opportunity on casual clothes. Clearly, Claudia was having a hard time reconciling fashion conscious me with ass-kicking me.

She shook her head. "A pretty girl like you shouldn't fight." She gave my arm a little squeeze before reaching for the bolt of fabric I'd set aside and handing it back to me. "You should stick to sewing."

If only that were an option. I smiled ruefully. "I really should."

Content with my answer, she moved back to the counter. "You tell me if there is anything you cannot find. Yes?"

I nodded and went back to stacking supplies on the counter. Even though I had come to Romania to learn how to control the demon now tethered to my soul, I still had a business to run. Emma was manning my shop in my absence, but without new inventory, I wouldn't be able to keep the doors open when I returned. Demon or no demon, I'd spent too long building my dream to sacrifice it now. Thanks to the Kansas City Renaissance Festival and haunted house season, September through November brought in enough business to keep The Costume Shoppe afloat for the rest of the year. With seven weeks until busy season hit, I crammed my evenings with marathon costume construction sessions while devoting my days to brutal training sessions with Aleksei's crew.

On impulse, I grabbed a couple of metallic glitter paint pens and a roll of cute washi tape from the craft section of the store and added them to my growing pile. I had just started rifling through Claudia's fabulous stock of vintage buttons when I felt the flutter of wings against my chest.

As soon as I'd arrived at the Compound, I had demanded Aleksei teach me how to wall myself off from the demon now masquerading as a crow tattooed over my heart. I wanted an off switch, but of course, it wasn't that simple. Most days, I kept the connection locked down so that the demon was little more than an irritant itching under my skin. But there were times like this when Raum clawed his way to the surface. Although the crow tattoo was covered by my shirt, its dark presence pulsed with warning.

I looked up, tensing as a man stepped into the shop. He wasn't the sort who frequented a place like this. Short and stocky, he was a little paunchy around the middle. His expression made it clear he was looking for a fight. He stilled when he spotted me, and his lips pulled back into a nasty smile. I didn't have to see red in his eyes to know he was a vampire.

Claudia stepped between us, partially blocking my view. "Can I help you?" she asked the man.

While he was temporarily sidelined by Claudia, I catalogued potential escape routes. I had no doubt he was here for me. What I didn't know was whether he'd come to kill me or take me to Wallace Ratcliff III, the master vampire who had already attempted to take me out once. Only Aleksei's intervention and the Enclave's protection had saved me then. Today, I was on my own.

With a vampire between me and the front door, I had two choices. I could fight my way past him or go out the back. Either way, a fight was inevitable, but going out the back would shift it away from Claudia and any innocent bystanders who happened to wander into her store. The demon practically hummed beneath my skin in anticipation of violence.

I scoured the shelves for anything I could turn into a makeshift weapon. Despite my pounding heart and my demon's anticipation, I forced myself to move unhurriedly toward the back exit. All the while, I kept my eyes trained on the vampire who was trying to push his way past a chattering Claudia. He was getting impatient, and I was afraid he'd hurt Claudia to get to me.

I grabbed a skein of yarn like I was still shopping and added a pair of size 10 circular bamboo knitting needles. I waved both in the air. "Claudia, could you be a dear and charge these to my tab with the rest of my purchase?"

I'd put a card on file the first week I'd come into her shop, so my request wasn't completely out of left field. Although she looked at me quizzically, she moved away from the vampire and headed behind the counter to note my purchases on the pad she kept next to the register. I dropped the yarn but kept the knitting needles. Without Claudia in the way, I could see the vamp's sneer as he strode down the aisle toward me.

Moving to the fabric counter, I pocketed the metal shears used to cut yards of material from the neatly wound bolts. Then, I knocked the mannequin dressed in a frilly smock into the man's path. "Oops!"

I pivoted and sprinted for the back door, sending a carousel of thread careening into the aisle as I passed it. I was going to have to do a lot of groveling to get back in Claudia's good graces after this—unless she assumed the guy barreling through her shop after me was the same guy who left the bruise on my cheek. In that case, she'd probably give me a pat on the back and an attagirl for taking her advice to heart.

The urge to look over my shoulder grew, but I didn't look back as I shoved the door open and ran outside. I quickly scanned the alley, relieved to find it empty. Inside, the vampire had eyed me like prey, which meant he would be expecting me to run for the safety of the busy street around the corner. I was banking on it, in fact. Even after three weeks under Aleksei's tutelage, my greatest asset was that my opponents unfailingly underestimated me. The element of surprise was no small thing in a fight.

I am your greatest asset, girl, Raum's voice whispered in my head. After a couple weeks of intensive training, I was better at shutting the demon down, but whenever strong emotions surged, or my focus slipped, Raum was there waiting to break through.

Ignoring him, I tucked my stolen shears in the back waistband of my pants for easier access. Then, I ripped the knitting needles out of their packaging and stretched the nylon cord tight. I stepped to the side of the door and flattened myself against the wall, trying to rein in the bloodlust leeching through my bond. I didn't have to wait long.

As he stepped outside, the vampire paused to scan down alley, which gave me enough time to move in behind him. Before he could stop me, I looped the cord around his beefy neck and yanked the bamboo knitting needles until the cord was taut against his throat. Then, I tightened my grip on both knitting needles and dropped my weight, using the cord like piano wire.

On instinct, his hands clawed at his neck, but the cord was too tight for him to get a hand on it. Unless I could manage to decapitate him—unlikely with nylon cord—it wouldn't kill him, though. The best I could hope for was cutting off his air supply long enough to render him unconscious, giving me enough time to get out of Dodge before he woke back up.

The vamp gave up trying to pry my makeshift garrote from his throat and threw a hard elbow into my chest. Fortunately, the angle was off enough he didn't crack my rib cage. But it still hurt like a bitch. Despite the pain, I held on, twisting my body so my shoulder would take the brunt of any future blows.

Just as the fight was leaving his body, and I was beginning to believe I'd walk away alive, two more vampires appeared to block the end of the alley. *Great.* Unlike the man slumping in my arms, these two were big and built for fighting. I let the vamp I'd just choked out slide to the ground as the two newcomers came for me.

My hands shook as I reached for the shears tucked into my waistband, but I didn't pull them out yet, hoping for the element of surprise. My crow tattoo flickered to life again, promising me the strength of a demon if only I'd reach for it.

Ignoring the temptation, I held my left hand up in front of me while I gripped the shears behind my back in my right.

"Listen, guys, I'm not looking for any trouble." I edged closer to the street, stopping while there was still plenty of space between us.

The bigger of the two smiled at me. "You hear that, Grif? She's not looking for any trouble."

His buddy didn't answer. He stared pointedly at the vamp crumpled on the street, my knitting needles still dangling from his neck. *It isn't my fault that trouble keeps finding me.* I swallowed and gripped the shears tighter in my fist. Neither of the men spoke, but they moved in perfect synchronization. The big guy stepped back and positioned himself in the middle of the alley, cutting off any hope of an easy escape.

Tall, dark, and quiet struck hard and fast. One second, he was studying me without a hint of emotion, and the next, he was going for my throat. I barely had enough time to react. I brought my arm up before driving the shears into the side of his head with all my strength. Even with a pair of sewing scissors buried in his ear, the man didn't make a sound. He did let go of me long enough to pull them back out, giving me the opening I needed to run for the street.

Don't look. Don't look, I chanted in my head as I ran past him. I had a queasy stomach, and that sight was guaranteed to be gross.

The big guy was ready and waiting. He opened his arms and smiled, prepared to lunge for my body as I darted toward him. Instead of trying to get past him as he expected, I dropped my shoulder and rammed it into his gut while wrapping my arms around the back of his tree-trunk thighs. Despite his size, the element of surprise worked in my favor, and I got him off his feet. He slammed into the pavement.

You should kill him, Raum said without inflection, like he was reminding me to pick up milk on the way home.

I scrambled away from the vampire instead, not because I was opposed to killing a vampire who'd attacked me, but because I didn't have the means or the time to see the job done. Adrenaline roared through my veins as I surged past him, and for the second time, I thought I'd make it.

The blow to the back of my head dashed those hopes before I could make it out of the alley. I staggered but kept my feet under me. The stumble cost me, though. It slowed me enough for the vampire I'd just dropped to get a hand on my ankle and yank my foot out from under me. I landed hard on my back, my head bouncing against the ground. My sight grew hazy, the sounds of the nearest busy street fading into a din that echoed in my aching head.

I didn't pass out, but battling the pain and disorientation was enough to distract me from the iron lock I kept on my control. When Raum's power surged, I didn't fight him. My tattoo warmed, and my vision narrowed to a bird's-eye view. I was no longer in the alley, but somewhere else.

Darkness edged my sight, directing my attention like the sight on a sniper's rifle to the man who walked with confidence down a dimly lit street. Despite not knowing who I was tailing, panic rose in my chest as I watched him. *Something bad will happen here.*

I was behind him, so I couldn't see his face, but I couldn't shake the sense that I knew him. The man was tall and muscular, his hair cut tight to his scalp. He was wearing gym clothes and had a duffle bag thrown over one shoulder. As I watched the man walk, I recognized the way he spun his keychain around his index finger. I didn't have to see his face. I'd walked behind that swagger most of my life. *Drew.*

Although I couldn't hear a sound, he must have heard something to make him pause and tilt his head to listen. His body tensed as if anticipating an attack. My gaze snapped to the left, where something moved in the shadow of the building.

I watched as Frederick Masterson stepped out of the shadows, his lips moving to compel his victim. As a silent bystander to this vision, there was nothing I could do but observe as Drew stiffened. He dropped the duffle bag he carried to the sidewalk and turned toward Masterson.

The distant streetlight illuminated his features so I could see my brother's face clearly. Drew obediently stood in front of Masterson, waiting for the dagger in Masterson's hand to cut his wrist. I couldn't move, and I couldn't scream. All I could do was watch as Masterson held a vial below the vein he'd sliced open and filled it with my brother's blood.

Masterson looked directly at me, like he could sense me there, even in a vision. Then, he tossed my brother aside and smiled. His eyes were the pitch black of a demon, telling me Beleth was in control as he watched Drew's body crumple to the ground. Masterson stood between me and a clear view of my brother. When he finally stepped away from Drew, the vision flickered like an old television set, and I woke to blackness.

Terror at the vision pounded through me. I had no way of knowing whether Masterson had left my brother dead or alive. All I knew for certain was that Beleth was coming for me, and he was going to use my family to do it.

CHAPTER 2

"**S**he's coming to." The voice came from above me.

Crap. The vision had distracted me from the immediate danger of the vampires who'd attacked me. I felt a presence looming over me, even though I couldn't see. I blinked several times, my eyes dry and gritty, but I still couldn't see a thing. Strong hands grabbed my shoulders, shaking me until my teeth rattled.

"You awake there, princess?"

It was the mocking nickname that gave him away. "You've got to be kidding me. This was all a fucking drill?"

No one answered me. I lay still, trying to blink away the darkness, to no avail. I reached a hand up and felt the all-too-familiar hood that covered my face, confirmation that the vampires sent to attack me had been yet another of Aleksei's training ops. I knew better than to remove the hood necessary to safeguard the location of the Compound, so I sat in darkness and fumed.

"I need a phone. Now."

One of the men chuckled. "Not likely. But don't worry."

The voice was mocking. "Grif went back for your craft supplies."

"Just get me back to the Compound."

No one else spoke on the long drive. The minute the van slowed to a stop, I was on my feet, shuffling my way to the door. Before I could step down, one of the men hoisted me over his shoulder, hood still firmly in place.

"I can walk, you know."

"Maybe I like carrying you," the man holding me joked.

I tried to wiggle free, but his arm was a tight band across the back of my thighs.

"Seriously, put me down," I demanded, clutching my hands together and bringing them down as hard as I could on the small of his back.

He grunted and shifted my weight, but he kept walking. "Relax, princess. You took a nasty blow back there." There was no apology in his voice.

"So did you," I countered. I wasn't sure which of the vamps had me, but I'd landed hits to both of them before I went down.

He slapped the back of my thigh as he laughed. "Touché."

By the time he slid me to the ground, I had a stomachache from all the bouncing against his shoulder and a simmering rage at the games Aleksei liked to play in the name of training. When the hood was jerked off, it didn't surprise me to find myself face-to-face with the devil himself.

Unlike the rest of the Compound's staff, who dressed uniformly in black combat gear, Aleksei wore a soft gray suit with a white button-down shirt more expensive than my shop rent back in Kansas City. If you didn't look into the dead weight of his eyes, you'd think him out of place in an institution that trained the world's deadliest assassins and spies.

I clenched my fists, tamping down the urge to throw a punch at Aleksei's face for sending vampires to a sewing shop to attack me. Right now, I had more urgent matters to attend to. "I need to call my brother."

Aleksei raised a dark eyebrow. "No phone calls."

"He's in danger." My pulse hammered as I pictured the blank look on Drew's face as he obeyed Masterson without a fight. "Please."

Aleksei's expression remained impassive. "Come."

I trailed after him hopefully as he led me away from the constant din of fighting that filled the courtyard. He opened the door to his office and invited me inside. The room felt about as welcoming as any good old boys' club space could, with its old-world masculine dark walls and broken-in leather furniture. Although I'd never seen him smoke, cigars perfumed the air.

He shut the door and gestured for me to take a seat. The chair he'd offered was situated facing his massive oak desk and—probably by design—it sat several inches lower than the executive chair behind the desk. Since there wasn't a phone on his desk, I bypassed the chair next to it and dropped into one of the leather wingback chairs instead. Aleksei's lips quirked at my minor defiance, but he moved the matching chair around, so we'd be facing each other.

I didn't wait for him to settle in before I repeated my demand. "I need to call my brother."

"So you said." Aleksei studied me with those uncanny pale blue eyes of his. "What makes you think he's in danger?"

"I saw him."

Aleksei leaned forward in interest. "In your vision?"

I tensed. "How do you know I had a vision?"

"Your eyes."

"What about my eyes?"

Pure demons, like Zepar had been, could shift their eyes to pits of black, which was terrifying to behold. When they became vampires, their eyes turned red to indicate strong emotion—usually rage—and bloodlust. It was why vampires' eyes flashed red before they attacked. Vampires were little more than demons walking around in human skin. Demons bonded to the human soul moments before it left its dying body, with the demon taking over the body and suppressing the soul. Thus far, I had been able to wrestle control of my soul despite Raum taking up residence, so I was something different—something new. It was hard to say what color my eyes would turn under duress.

But I'd lost control back in that alley, even if it had only been a momentary lapse. "Did my eyes turn red?" I asked, afraid of the answer.

"Not red." Aleksei's expression grew somber. "Griffin said your eyes turned milky white when the vision hit you. He said it was unsettling." He grimaced. For a vamp to call it unsettling, I must have been quite the sight. "You stayed that way for a good ten minutes, Kali. Your body was rigid and your eyes fixed open."

I shivered, imagining what I must have looked like. It hadn't felt like I had been caught in the vision for that long.

"Is this the first vision you've had?" Aleksei asked.

"Like this, yes. Early on, I'd sometimes get flashes of images, but they were more like memories." I met Aleksei's eyes. "Since you taught me how to shut down the bond, I haven't had any more of those. Even when I did, they were nothing like this vision."

"How was this one different?"

The vision replayed in my head as I described it. "For

starters, this one tunneled my vision through the crow's eyes, just like when I've called on the crow in the past. There was a certain detachment to this one, like I was watching what happened as a spectator."

Aleksei leaned back in his chair. "Tell me about this vision."

"I saw a man—my brother—walking down a dark street. Someone was waiting for him, ready to attack. At first, I couldn't see who it was. But when he stepped into the light, I recognized Frederick Masterson." I recounted the vision, describing it in as much detail as I could recall, as much to commit it to my own memory as to convey it to Aleksei. "Masterson slit Drew's wrist and took a vial of his blood."

"You're positive it was Masterson?" Aleksei asked. Having been briefed on what occurred in Kansas City, he already knew that, like me, Masterson was bonded to a demon —Beleth.

Instead of handing over a phone immediately, as I'd hoped, Aleksei continued to question me. "What about the location? Did you recognize where this occurred?"

I shook my head. "No."

"Close your eyes," Aleksei commanded. "Try to recreate the scene from your memory."

I obeyed, concentrating on the vision. This time, I focused on his surroundings. The street was a residential one, but not one I recognized. The houses were modest and crowded together, and the area was poorly lit. The cracked sidewalk indicated an older, working-class neighborhood, and the density of the housing said it was a city. Because of the darkness that blanketed the street, I couldn't make out any defining details that could identify it as Chicago. I conveyed all of that to Aleksei before opening my eyes.

"You said the man carried a duffle bag?" Aleksei asked.

"Yes. Based on how he was dressed, I'm guessing he was coming from or going to a workout."

"Most likely," Aleksei agreed. "Did you see a gym?"

I let out a frustrated breath. "No, but I'll be sure to ask Drew where he works out when I talk to him."

Aleksei ignored me, continuing to probe at my memory of the vision. "Concentrate on whatever it was that your brother heard."

"There was no sound in the vision." Whatever sound tipped him off to Masterson lurking in the shadows hardly seemed important. What mattered was that every second I sat here recounting the vision was another second my brother was in danger. I stood and started pacing the floor. "I need to call Drew right now to warn him."

Aleksei steepled his fingers and watched me pace, displaying not a shred of concern. "And tell him what?"

I paused my pacing and faced Aleksei. "That he's in danger."

"And when he asks about what kind of danger, what will you say? That a demon gave you a vision of him being attacked by a man possessed by another demon?"

"I'll make something up." I racked my brain for a plausible story. "I'll describe Masterson and say he's a stalker who threatened to target my family."

Even as I said it, I knew it would never work. If Drew thought I had a stalker, he would go into hyper-protective mode and be on the first plane to Kansas City. If I managed to get there by the time he arrived, he'd grill me for hours and run every detail I gave him through the system. It would be a colossal waste of time, and in the end, Drew wouldn't be any safer than if I'd said nothing. I sat back down in my chair.

Giving Drew a vague warning to watch his back wasn't going to work, and honestly, a normal human wouldn't see Masterson coming from a mile away, even with a warning. None of us had.

Aleksei sat silently, waiting for me to come to the same conclusion he had when I demanded a phone. Maybe my brother wouldn't take my warning seriously, but I knew one person who would.

I sat back down. "Then I need to talk to Craig."

Aleksei stared at me. "No."

One of the rules of the Compound was no cell phones or other electronics that could be used to contact the outside world. Since arriving three weeks ago, I hadn't spoken to Emma, Craig, or Riley. The only way to get into contact with someone outside these walls was to go through Aleksei, and he'd made it abundantly clear that radio silence was expected for the duration of my training. However, this was an emergency.

"Yes," I countered. "I need to call Craig." I wasn't budging on this. Craig needed to know about my vision. If there was any possibility of preventing it from happening, I needed to try.

Aleksei didn't say anything for a long time, and I held out hope he could be swayed—a hope that was quickly dashed. "I'll contact Craig."

I dug my heels in. "I need to talk to him myself."

Aleksei's eyes flashed amber. "Don't push me, *ptichka*."

I gritted my teeth at the nickname. Last week, I'd bribed one of the Russian guards to tell me what it meant, sure it was something pejorative. The guard told me it meant "little bird," and I hated that more than the perceived insult.

I scanned his body, wondering if he kept a cell phone on

him. "You must have a phone somewhere." When we'd come to the Compound to interrogate Naomi months ago, Aleksei had handed me a business card with a lone phone number on it. People didn't hand out phone numbers without the phones to answer them.

"None that you can use," Aleksei said easily.

"What if there's a fire?" I asked conversationally. "You must have a way to call the fire department."

"We have water elementals on staff."

"Okay, well, what if someone has a heart attack while training, and you need to call an ambulance?"

Aleksei leaned closer to me, his breath brushing over my cheek. "Then, we bury him." Before I could argue further, Aleksei held up his hand. "I will relay everything you've said to Craig. I'll also notify the Enclave so they can assign Shadows to watch over your brother." He leaned back in his seat as if the matter were settled. "Now, back to your demon. He's supposed to possess visions of the past, present, and future." Aleksei stared at me expectantly. "Which was this?"

I thought about it, but I had no way of determining the time frame from what I'd seen. "I have no idea," I admitted.

"Until we know that, it's hard to say what the vision means or when—or even if—it will occur. It could be fictional images to manipulate your emotions."

Aleksei's frown said he didn't believe the vision was fictional any more than I did. I knew firsthand what it was like to have a demon manipulate my emotions, and this vision rang true. And even if it wasn't, I couldn't take the risk.

Aleksei stretched his long legs in front of him and rested his arm on the chair. His casual stance didn't fool me. Aleksei only feigned casual when he was angling for a confession. "Other than this one vision, the only times you've felt connected to Raum is when you either used the crow to spy or got flashes of memories, correct?"

When I'd first arrived at the Compound, Aleksei had grilled me for hours about how the demon felt and how I'd used his powers. Because I was desperate to learn how to control Raum, I hadn't held anything back from him. The only thing Aleksei didn't know was the most recent development—the insidious voice that sometimes whispered in my head.

Don't tell him, Raum warned.

I took a deep breath and blurted it out before I lost my nerve. "Lately, I've been hearing Raum's voice in my head. Not all the time, but when I feel strong emotions, like fear or rage, he gains a foothold and can speak to me."

Aleksei's eyes narrowed. "What does he tell you?"

"Mostly to hide things or to kill people he views as threats to me," I confessed. "But I've always been able to shut him out quickly."

Aleksei got a calculating look on his face that I'd come to dread. He stood abruptly. "Let's see what happens when you aren't so quick to shut him down."

I paled and sunk deeper into my chair. The last thing I wanted to do was encourage Raum's running monologue in my head. "That seems like a bad idea."

Before I could object further, Aleksei pulled me to my feet and propelled me out his door. "The better we understand this vision, the more likely we will be able to protect your brother. Who better to help us understand it than Raum?"

I crossed my arms and planted my feet. "First, call Craig and the Enclave."

Aleksei bent down until our faces were even. "When I have

extracted all the information about the vision, I will make my calls."

I grimaced. Extracting information didn't sound like a friendly chat. Aleksei turned his back on me and walked down the hall, confident I'd follow.

"Where are we going?" I called after him.

"To train."

"We're going the wrong way," I objected. The courtyard was in the opposite direction.

Aleksei kept walking, only pausing when we reached my room. "Go put on something more appropriate," he said.

I glanced down at my cute top. "What's wrong with what I'm wearing?" *Talking to a demon doesn't exactly require a track suit.*

He scowled at my choice of outfit. "Training clothes. Two minutes," he warned, glancing at his watch as I opened the door.

I snorted. *Who changes clothes in two minutes?* "Five."

"One minute," he countered.

"Fine," I snapped. "Two minutes."

CHAPTER 3

*L*ike a Pavlovian response, my breath quickened as we neared the quad of rooms unaffectionately dubbed Purgatory. Aleksei stopped in front of a large wall of observation windows. Although combat practice took place in the open courtyard, these windows showcased where the most grueling training took place. Unlike the sore muscles and bruised ribs I acquired during martial arts instruction and weapons training, this was where I had learned to close off the demon who had wormed his way into my soul.

The cavernous space was divided into four training areas. One-quarter of the room was dedicated to containment cells equipped to handle the strongest out-of-control shifters and rabid vampires. Next to the cells was the infirmary, where I'd already been patched up a couple times during my stay. Another area held the tank—an oversized containment cell lined with a metal floor perfect for conducting low-wattage electrical currents and a ceiling dotted with nozzles capable of drenching occupants with either water or knock-out gas.

One afternoon within the confines of the tank was all it took for me to lock down my demon on command.

Aleksei led me to the section of the room I hadn't yet ventured into. This area was a classic example of one of these things not being like the others. Whereas the rest of the room was lit with harsh fluorescent fixtures and fitted with utilitarian surfaces, this corner was lit softly. Heavy brocade curtains draped from the ceiling, giving the illusion that this space was separate from the rest of the room. Thick, interlocking gym mats softened the floor, and throw pillows the color of sand and sky were scattered around the edges. It looked more like a yoga retreat than a Compound training area, but I'd been here long enough that it would take more than a few pillows and mood lighting to fool me. Softness was an illusion in this world.

Even after three weeks of daily training, my heart rate still sped up in anticipation. Aleksei kicked off his expensive Italian loafers before stepping onto the mat. He held the curtain aside for me and waited. I followed his lead, my pulse jackhammering in my wrist as he dropped the curtain behind me.

He gazed down at me, frowning. "You need to learn to control your heart rate. You sound like a frightened rabbit." Given his enhanced shifter senses, it didn't surprise me that Aleksei had picked up on my nervousness. There was no censure in his voice, but the downturn of his lips made it clear he found my inability to control my fight-or-flight response disappointing. He didn't wait for a reply. "Sit."

I hesitated. "Why?"

He glared at me. "Sit." This time, he barked the command, reminding me of his brother. Normally, Aleksei hid behind a persona of cultured, albeit deadly, sophistication, but beneath that veneer, he was still a Volkov.

I lowered myself cautiously to the ground, keeping Aleksei in my line of sight. He looked beyond the curtain and flicked his wrist. Someone dimmed the lights further, and the speakers piped in the sound of waves lapping against a shoreline. None of it relaxed me. I sat stiff-backed, waiting for Aleksei to drop his bomb.

He grabbed a folding chair from where it leaned against a wall and sat it a few feet in front of me. I didn't miss the stun baton he took from the wall, bracing it across his lap as he sat. Once seated, Aleksei looked at me expectantly. "It's time you stopped avoiding Raum. You need to have better control over this demon, or he'll swallow you whole."

Arguing would be pointless. Just because the space around me looked like a yoga retreat didn't mean Aleksei would limit himself to ocean sounds to coax the demon out. Calling on Raum might be the last thing I wanted to do, but I was willing to do anything that could help protect my family from Masterson.

"Fine," I bit out.

Aleksei relaxed into his chair as if what we were doing wasn't terrifying. "Good. Let's begin. I want you to close your eyes and concentrate on the bond."

I was not the meditation type. I preferred to keep my hands busy and my mind spinning. When I'd first moved to Kansas City, I'd let Emma convince me to go to a meditative yoga session she'd been raving about. I spent an hour resisting the urge to itch my nose while periodically staring at the people in front of me through my eyelashes. All I got out of it was a sore ass and a deep dislike for ambient music.

"Concentrate," Aleksei ordered.

After a few minutes of fidgeting, I managed to tune out the sounds of the medical equipment and hum of conversation, so I could focus on Aleksei's meditation playlist. *I hope when this is all said and done, I don't develop an aversion to the ocean.* As I finally began to relax, the creak of the metal folding chair jarred me.

I cracked an eye open to see what he was doing.

Aleksei leaned forward enough to rest the stun baton against my thigh. "Close your eyes," he ordered.

Not wanting to give him an excuse to zap me, I closed my eyes.

"Now, find the point you've pinched closed and open it up again." At my huff of annoyance, Aleksei pitched his voice low and smooth, like he was coaxing a frightened animal to eat from his hand. "Find the connection, Kali."

People only attempt handfeeding a wild animal when they are about to cage it, I thought, remembering the shock of the baton the first time one of the trainers used it.

"You can open the pathway and still retain control. You're stronger than he is."

I wasn't convinced, but sooner or later, I was going to have to test that theory. Better to test it here with Aleksei waiting in a room full of tools to knock me out should I lose control.

As I focused on the soul bond, even the sound of waves receded into silence. I concentrated first on my tattoo, picturing the black-winged crow peering at me among surrounding tree branches laden with even more crows. Zeroing in on the largest crow, I met his eyes and watched awareness flicker there. Then, I followed the ink into my skin, feeling it tunnel into my body until it wove around my soul. My stomach pitched as I studied it—saw how the demon had fused with my soul. Just beyond the fusion was the pinch point that allowed me to block the demon.

I didn't know how exactly I was supposed to open the connection, so I did the only thing I could think of. I imagined the pinch point expanding, like letting up on a garden hose I'd clamped shut in my fist. I didn't let up entirely, but it opened the connection enough that I felt Raum's presence leaching into me. For a second, I panicked and clamped down again.

The next time I released the pressure, I was ready for him. I focused on the feel of the demon as his power infused my body. Zepar was the only other demon I had experience with, but Raum felt nothing like him. There was still the pull of dark power, but it didn't feel as insidious. I let it in, bit by bit, until I sensed the tipping point. Raum's emotions swelled within me until it was hard to tell where my rage ended and his fuel of it began.

Let me show you what we are capable of, he coaxed, filling my body with a strength I'd never known.

As a woman tired of being underpowered in a world that valued strength, the feeling was intoxicating, and I reveled in it. My control began slipping.

Yes. That's it, he whispered.

This time, I barely managed to ratchet the connection down. Although fear at losing control made me want to quit, I kept going. I tried again and again, discovering where the precipice was and learning to walk that razor's edge. *I can do this,* I thought.

Thousands of volts of electricity sizzling through my body was Aleksei's way of signaling the end of the exercise. When I got my breathing and the demon under control, I stared at the baton in Aleksei's hands. "What the hell is wrong with you?"

Instead of looking contrite, Aleksei shrugged an Armani-clad shoulder and smiled at me. "You needed a little nudge, *ptichka.*"

"You wanted the demon to take control," I accused.

"No. I wanted to see if you could maintain control under pressure." Aleksei set the stun baton on the floor when he saw me fixating on it. "You did well."

Thanks a lot, asshole. I glared at him.

"Now it's time to interrogate your little demon." Aleksei made Raum sound like a pet Pomeranian. "Open the bond again, only this time, see if you can coax him into a conversation. Ease into the questions about the vision." Aleksei leaned forward, his expression serious. "Do not say anything he could construe as a binding agreement. Do you understand?"

I wiped my sweaty palms on my pants. "Yes."

"This time, you need to do it with your eyes open," Aleksei instructed. "You'll need to be able to tap into the demon's powers and communicate when under attack."

I took a few seconds to settle, then opened the connection. I waited until I felt Raum's presence swelling under my skin and the flutter of wings against my chest. Rather than starting with inane small talk, I waited for Raum to speak first. It didn't take long.

You should use the weapon on him, Raum insisted, showing me an image of Aleksei's stun baton.

For once, we were in perfect agreement. *Maybe someday.* I projected the thought. Since I hadn't tried responding to any of Raum's previous suggestions of murder and mayhem, I wasn't entirely sure he'd be able to hear me. When a sense of dark satisfaction filled me, I had my answer. *Right now, I could use your help.* As soon as the thought formed, I recognized my error even before he responded.

We will help each other, Raum said.

I swallowed. Plotting with a demon was a slippery slope, but the memory of Drew's body at Masterson's feet was enough to make me continue. Hearing Raum out wasn't the same as agreeing. *What do you want?*

He hummed with excitement. *You will be the destroyer, and I will illuminate your path.* An image rose in my mind of a demon with onyx horns that curled against his skull. While most demons' eyes were pitch black, this demon's eyes were elongated like a cat's and flecked with hellfire. I trembled as I looked upon him.

Is that you? I whispered, terrified of the thing inside me. *How could I control something like that?*

I felt Raum's anger rise as my own. *I show you the face of the false king. He thinks to use us, but together, we will kill him.*

I felt Raum tug on the bond, edging me aside so he could take control. I cranked the valve, shifting the balance of power back into my hands. *Beleth.* I meant it as a question, even though it didn't come out that way.

Beleth, Raum agreed.

I'd read enough demonology texts to know better than to outright agree to a demon's demands. *I want Beleth dead as much as you. But first, I need to understand the vision you sent me of Masterson—Beleth,* I corrected—*attacking my brother in order to find me.*

He must not find you before we have the means to kill him, Raum said. *But I do not control the visions.*

How can I tell when the events from a vision will happen? If I could predict when the attack would occur, it would be easier to prevent.

Raum dashed my hopes. *Visions can be something that will be or something that has been. Sometimes they are what is. There is no distinction between the visions when they come.*

It hadn't occurred to me I could be seeing something that had already come to pass, and terror clawed its way up my throat. Raum fed from it, growing stronger the more out of control I felt. I shoved the possibility from my head, telling myself that I would know if my brother was already dead. I forced myself to ask the question I feared the answer to. *Are the visions absolute, or can the events they show be changed?*

Raum was quiet long enough that I was afraid I'd lost the connection. *Visions are but one path. Altering the path does not always change the outcome in the way we wish.* A wave of regret washed over me, and I was certain it came from Raum.

I'll take my chances, I told him. But I knew even if I managed to circumvent this vision, Beleth would keep coming for me, putting everyone I loved in danger. *Tell me how to kill Beleth.*

Instead of answering in words, Raum sent me a memory filled with smoke and hellfire. As the smoke cleared, I found myself in the middle of a battlefield. Bodies littered the ground, most of them bearing the marks of teeth and claw. These had not been quick deaths, and some of the demons had left tracks on the dusty ground where they had dragged themselves out of the melee toward a safety they never reached. The fighting was all around me, but I floated above it. From my vantage point, I could take in the sheer mass of the destruction.

Demons warred on foot and on mounts. Unlike the wars of men, they didn't dig into trenches or bomb the enemy from afar. Demons fought like barbarians, their expressions euphoric as they tore through the bodies of their enemies. Although I tried to sort the demons into enemy camps, there were no uniforms to mark the side they fought for.

On the far side of the field, the horde parted to make way

for a demon king. On his head, he wore a black crown dotted with fire gemstones. The demon king hadn't come on a war horse, and his towering frame was more terrifying because of it. Even on foot, he was massive, nearing eight feet tall at least.

He carried a war scythe in one hand and raised his other clawed fist in the air before reaching behind him to pull a shield from his back, the blood red crest painted on it vaguely familiar. When he charged, the demons facing him didn't stand a chance. He cut them down and moved on without sparing their dismembered bodies another glance. He was brutality personified, and I trembled in his wake. All around him trumpets blared, the upbeat music a cheery contrast to the horror all around me.

Find his weapons and kill the king, Raum's voice whispered in my head.

How do I do that? I asked.

Bring me the orb, and we will scry for them, he said.

What orb?

There was a slight pause before Raum answered, projecting his voice loud enough that I winced. *The Orb of Raum the Almighty.*

Did you just make that up? I scoffed.

We could make it stick. He sounded defensive. When I didn't respond, he showed me a small glass orb the size of a snow globe. The glass was clear except for the living flames that danced inside it.

I don't suppose you know where to find this orb, do you?

The only answer was the melody of Beleth's war trumpets that heralded the death and destruction sure to come. Even if I managed to find the orb and secure his weapons, I wondered how many of us would be left standing when this was over.

CHAPTER 4

As far as cryptic visions went, a demon war felt pretty damn ominous. I consoled myself that as terrifying as a battle-honed Beleth was, it had only been a memory. At least he'd been surrounded by hellfire and not blue skies and the Chicago or Kansas City skyline—for now, at least.

Despite recounting my disturbing internal conversation with Raum, Aleksei still refused to lend me a phone to contact Craig myself. Without knowing when Masterson would go after Drew, the urgency to get protection in place for him overwhelmed me. Aleksei, however, deemed sharing the new information about Beleth with the Enclave to be the priority.

"One phone call," I begged. I trailed after Aleksei as he made his way to the courtyard armory, where he chose an assortment of knives and guns to strap to his body in preparation for venturing outside the Compound walls. "That's all I'm asking for. Give me ten minutes to talk to Craig."

"No." Aleksei didn't stop to look at me, tucking a knife into an ankle holster beneath his pant leg. "I've already told you that I will request Shadows be assigned to protect your brother."

Because the Enclave had a strict no direct contact rule, Aleksei had to go through an intermediary. While the all-powerful Enclave may be content with painfully slow communication channels, I was not. Aleksei ignored my continued protests as he went to meet the Enclave's representative at an undisclosed secure location, leaving me behind to cool my heels. If he knew me better, he wouldn't have left me unsupervised.

It didn't take long for me to convince Liv to help me break into the secure communications room, so I could call home. After several weeks without a mission, she was bored and ready to stir up some trouble, which suited my needs perfectly.

"Are you sure there isn't another way to get into the comms room?" I asked Liv as we eyed the heavy steel door that required both a fingerprint and retinal ID to enter. We were at the end of the corridor directly under the security camera where we were out of sight. If Riley had been here, she'd have come up with some way to bypass the scanners without having to resort to convincing someone to let us in.

Liv elbowed me in the side. "Stop worrying. Our plan is foolproof."

I snorted. Sweet-talking the tech guy into letting us in hardly constituted a foolproof plan. I looked up at the security camera. "You're sure we don't need to disable this somehow?"

Liv shook her head. "Nah. The only person monitoring the feed is the guy inside."

"The same tech guy you're going to convince to let us in."

"That would be the one." Liv rolled up the sleeves of her

shirt and grabbed the stack of paper she'd brought along. She wadded several sheets into balls. As a fire elemental, Liv rarely passed up an opportunity to light something on fire. Knocking on the door would have been easier, but it would have also given the guy inside time to call Aleksei before coming to the door. At least, that's how Liv convinced me that lobbing flaming balls of paper down the hall was a good idea.

"Fire in the hole," she shouted as she threw them one at a time.

By the fourth fireball, a frazzled-looking guy sporting horn-rimmed glasses and a scowl yanked the door open. He came out brandishing a fire extinguisher and a bad attitude. "Are you a moron?"

Liv pointed at him and then herself. "Pot meet kettle."

"Huh?" He scrunched his brow and stared at her as she stepped into his personal space.

They were almost the same height, which came in handy when Liv slipped behind him and put the poor guy in a head-lock. He raised the fire extinguisher like a weapon, but given their positions, the most he could do was wave it around.

"Settle down." She waited for him to tire himself out.

"What do you want?"

Liv grinned at me. "We're gonna need you to open that door, so Kali here can make a quick phone call to her boo."

He attempted to shake his head but didn't have the range of movement to pull it off. "No way. Aleksei would kill me."

Liv tightened her arm, cutting off his air supply.

I reached them just as his body slumped. "Don't hurt him."

She loosened her grip. "Get his hand."

I lifted his finger to the scanner and waited for the beep. Then, Liv pried his eyelid open and held him up to the retinal scanner. Seconds later, we were inside the comms room with a passed-out tech geek and a whole lot of high-tech equipment.

"Burner phones are over there." Liv propped the guy in an office chair like it was *Weekend at Bernie's* and pointed to a filing cabinet. "Top drawer."

I dialed Craig's emergency line by memory, not willing to waste this opportunity on a missed call. When Craig answered, my whole body relaxed.

Three weeks wasn't a long time, but I'd missed him. "It's good to hear your voice."

This was the first time I'd talked to anyone from home. Only Craig, Riley, and Max Volkov knew where I was. As far as the general public knew, I was out of town to spend time with an ailing great-aunt who didn't exist. Even the rest of the Tribunal had been kept in the dark about my exact location as a precaution.

"Are you okay?" He must have picked up on the little catch in my throat.

"I'm fine, but I need your help."

There was no hesitation. "Name it."

"I had a vision, courtesy of my demon tag-a-long. In it, I saw Masterson attack my brother."

Before I could say more, the door crashed open, and a very pissed off Aleksei stomped inside. He took one look at his tech guy, who was still out cold, and stalked over to me, holding out his hand for the phone.

"Well shit," Liv said. "I thought we'd have longer."

Unwilling to hand it over, I tucked my head to my neck and attempted to curl around the phone. It didn't take super-natural hearing to catch the growl rumbling out of Aleksei's chest.

"Kali, what's happening?" Craig demanded.

Aleksei grabbed the phone from my hand and put it to his ear. "She's fine, Ward." He met my eyes. "For now."

And now both of them were growling. Liv rolled her eyes and mimed peeing in a circle. When Aleksei turned her way, she mouthed "sorry" before making a hasty retreat out the still open door. The tech guy woke up, took one look at Aleksei's thunderous expression and paled.

"Leave us." Aleksei's voice was deceptively soft. The guy stumbled to his feet and wobbled after Liv.

While Aleksei was distracted, I reached for the phone again, but he held it in an iron grip. Aleksei waited for me to give up before putting the phone on speaker and gesturing for me to talk. I explained the situation in more detail. Aleksei interrupted to let us both know that the Enclave had agreed to assign Shadows to watch over Drew. They would be in place within twenty-four hours.

"What if he attacks before they get there?" Because Raum's visions could be about imminent events or things that would happen six months down the road, we had no idea when Masterson would attack Drew. He could be attacking him right now, for all we knew.

"I'll have my contacts check on him and cover him until then," Craig assured me.

"Thank you," I said, emotion clogging my throat.

Craig paused before jumping back to the vision. "You said that Masterson took a vial of Drew's blood, right?"

As soon as he pointed out that detail, I knew why. "You think he's going to attempt to find me using the tracking spell?"

"I do."

At the moment, Masterson had no idea where I was, only

that I wasn't in Kansas City. Because Masterson had the tracking spell from Samara's grimoire, all he needed to pinpoint my location was the blood from a descendant of my line.

I spun toward Aleksei. "I need to go home, now." As long as I was here, Drew was at risk. If I was home, Masterson would have no reason to go after Drew.

Aleksei stared down at me. "That won't be possible. With the new developments, you've been ordered to undergo evaluation before you can leave the premises unescorted."

"You've got to be kidding me."

Raum rumbled inside me as my anger grew. *We should feast on his entrails*, he suggested.

What is wrong with you? I scolded him before I turned to Aleksei. "You can't keep me here against my will."

"I can, and I will," Aleksei promised. Although Craig swore at him, Aleksei kept his attention on me. "We cannot risk setting you loose until we are confident that you can control Raum."

"I'm not feasting on your entrails, now am I?" I shot back.

"What?" Aleksei scowled at me.

"I'm just saying, that's probably what a demon would do." I kept the fact that Raum had been cheerleading for me to do just that to myself.

"You're going to have to prove that you can control him," Aleksei said. "In the meantime, your brother will be placed under the Enclave's protection, and my contact will convey the information Raum shared with you. If anyone can find the means to stop Masterson, it is the Enclave."

Craig's voice dropped dangerously low. "See that no harm comes to her."

"Done," Aleksei agreed, looking at me. "You have two minutes to finish this call."

I grabbed the phone and took it off speaker. Rather than wasting my two minutes rehashing things that couldn't be changed, I asked how everyone there was doing. Craig assured me he'd checked on Emma, and the shop was running smoothly in my absence, easing some of my tension.

"And Riley?" Normally, Riley and I didn't go more than a couple days without checking in. I missed bad movie nights and midnight donut runs. *Would my life ever settle into normalcy again?* I studied the scuffed toe of the ugly black boots I wouldn't have been caught dead wearing a few months ago. *Probably not.*

Craig didn't answer right away, and when he did, his tone was guarded. "I'm sure she's fine."

I sat up straighter. "What do you mean? You haven't seen her?"

"Not since the week you left," he admitted.

I groaned. Trouble might have a way of finding me, but as a goat shifter, Riley actively chased it. Going radio silent for three weeks wasn't like her. Something was wrong.

Craig cut in before I could spiral into full-blown panic. "I'll check on her," he promised.

"Thanks." I tried to tamp down my worry. For all I knew, she was binge-watching reality TV or recovering from a cold. Maybe she'd met a hot guy who was purging Max Volkov from her system. I perked up a little at that thought. It was probably fine. The last few months had me on edge. That was all.

When Craig was quiet on the other end of the line too long, my nerves kicked back in.

"What aren't you telling me?"

"I'm sure it's not connected," he assured me, "but there have been reports of supernaturals going missing."

I gripped the phone tighter. "What?"

"None have been reported missing in Kansas City, but another lower-level fire elemental disappeared from Nevada, and a wolf from an Iowa pack didn't come back from a routine patrol."

"When?"

"In the last week. Everyone's on high alert," he said.

"Except Riley." My voice shook with fear.

"Hey. Riley can handle herself, and she's not exactly the check-in type." I heard the jangling of keys and his truck door shutting. "I'm heading there now to make sure she's safe."

I breathed a little easier knowing he was headed her way. "Thanks."

Aleksei motioned for me to wrap up the call. I glared at him.

"Listen, I have to go, but I need to know she's okay."

Craig started his engine. "I'll get word to you."

I didn't ask how because I knew he'd find a way. "Okay."

"Stay safe, and if you need me…" he trailed off.

"I know. You, too."

Aleksei took the phone and tossed it back in the filing cabinet. "Your pink-haired friend is missing?" he asked.

He'd met Riley when we'd come to the Compound to meet with Naomi. Since he'd immediately picked up on whatever undercurrent was simmering between his brother and Riley, he'd naturally used it to needle Max. During their brief inter-action, he'd seemed to like Riley's signature take-no-shit attitude.

"Maybe," I acknowledged, worry creeping back in. "Craig is going to check to see."

Aleksei peered at me thoughtfully. "Lucky for you, I have just the thing to take your mind off it. Meet me in the courtyard in thirty minutes, and we'll get this evaluation started."

Fan-frickin-tastic. I had quickly learned that Aleksei and I had vastly different views of what constituted lucky.

CHAPTER 5

I choked down a few bites of a granola bar before tucking the rest in my pants pocket and heading out to meet Aleksei. Instead of the sparring practice I'd expected, he nodded to one of his soldiers, who shoved a hood over my head and took me to the van idling outside. I could have called on my crow to show me the route, but I let them keep their secrecy. At least they didn't bind my hands for this excursion. Of course, the guy hooding me had threatened a slow and painful death should I remove it, so we weren't exactly operating on the honor system, either.

Like usual, we drove for quite a while. I could never tell whether Aleksei instructed the driver to take the scenic route or if our destination was actually that far away. The location of the Compound was a closely guarded secret, and driving in mindless circles was a good way to ensure I couldn't retrace the route. Had they ever watched me attempt to navigate using a map and clear directions, they wouldn't have worried about me finding my way back.

When the van stopped, Aleksei jerked the hood from my head and nudged me toward the door.

"Where are we?" I asked suspiciously.

"Consider this your field test."

The last field test ended with me sprawled on the pavement with demon visions dancing in my head. I wasn't looking forward to this one.

Although the tail end of the drive had been rough, no amount of dips and bumps had prepared me for the wildness that surrounded us when I climbed out of the van. The whole area was overgrown with vegetation.

Aleksei stepped out behind me, taking stock of the landscape. He unbuttoned his suit jacket and took it off, folding it neatly before putting it in the back of the van. Standing there in his tailored pants, a crisp white button-down shirt, and a shoulder holster, he looked as ill-prepared for this place as I felt. Not that it phased him. Aleksei slammed the van door, the sound ominous.

Except for the open mouth of a tunnel and a crumbling stone building, the area looked more like a destination for an afternoon nature hike than a place to host a training exercise. I might have relaxed if it hadn't been for the razor wire barring the entrance to the tunnel. Unlike everything else here, it looked brand-spanking new. And that made me nervous. Thirty minutes was plenty of time for Aleksei's crew to retrofit that tunnel with all manner of nasty surprises.

The contingent of familiar faces milling around outside made me even more nervous. I counted three elite soldiers I recognized from the Compound, the big vamp who'd blocked my exit from the alley behind Claudia's store, and a dark-haired woman I'd never seen before. The big vamp gave me an assessing look before going back to setting out an assortment of medical supplies. *Well, that's not good.*

I turned my attention to the dark-haired woman, who flipped through a leather-bound grimoire until she found the page she was looking for. Witch. *That's really not good.*

"All set, sir," she called cheerfully to Aleksei before raking her gaze over me. She sneered and addressed the big vamp standing next to her. "It shouldn't take long before she taps out."

He didn't argue, but he didn't agree with her, either. I guess I'd made an impression earlier. *Go me.*

"There won't be any tapping out," Aleksei cut in.

Great. "What are we doing here?" I asked him.

Aleksei stepped up next to me, surveying the area. "Today is the day you demonstrate you can control your demon."

I eyed him skeptically. Controlling a demon didn't seem like something you mastered in a one-day kind of retreat. "How exactly do you propose I do that?"

Aleksei smiled. "With the proper motivation, anything is possible."

I squirmed. "Do I even want to know?" I mumbled.

"Probably not." He walked to the front of the van and motioned the others over. Everyone obeyed immediately, circling to the front of the van. Even our driver stood at attention, awaiting Aleksei's instructions. Reluctantly, I joined them.

Aleksei pointed toward the tunnel entrance. "Inside is the beginning of an obstacle course of sorts—one that will require you to use all the tools at your disposal to walk out of." He stared at the scoop neck of my shirt where my crow tattoo peeked out.

I shivered. It was an unseasonably cold day, with overcast

skies and a slight drizzle in the air. When Aleksei told me to meet him, I'd thrown on a black tank top, cargo pants, and the practical boots that had sadly become my go-to footwear. Had I known I was headed for an obstacle course in the bowels of the earth, I would have dressed in warmer clothes.

"Where does the tunnel lead?" Wherever it led, I was certain I wouldn't like venturing inside. As I stared at it, I saw movement. Whatever was in there, it was low to the ground. *Not human, then.*

Aleksei pointed beyond the tunnel to the remnants of a stone building buried under vines and overgrowth. "This is an abandoned military fort that was built in the nineteenth century to fortify Bucharest's defenses. It's connected to a hub of similar forts by tunnels, most of which have been abandoned for years."

"Wait." I stopped him. "You expect me to go into a two-hundred-year-old tunnel to get in touch with my inner demon?" My voice sounded shrill even to my own ears.

Aleksei took my outburst in stride. "Yes." When a couple of his soldiers chuckled, he cut them off with an irritated glance.

I pointed at the opening. "You expect me to go in the tunnel behind all that razor wire."

He stared at me as if I'd gone daft. "Yes," he repeated.

I crossed my arms over my chest. "That's ridiculous."

Aleksei shrugged. "Ridiculous or not, you're going in, and the only way you're coming out is by learning how to tap into the demon's powers." I watched the wolf rise, the amber in Aleksei's eyes a warning not to push him on this.

I swallowed. "I can't."

"Bullshit," he declared. "You're just afraid." When I didn't respond, he gripped my shoulders and turned my body to face him. "Listen to me, *ptichka.* Fear can be a good thing. It can keep you alive. But too much of it, and you freeze like a rabbit in the jaws of a wolf." I wondered if he was referring to himself because at this moment, I certainly felt like his teeth were at my neck. "Afraid or not, you need to learn how to use the demon to your advantage. That means drawing on his strength, using his enhanced senses, and compelling people when necessary." He read the objection in my body language before I could voice it and shook his head. "It will be necessary. If not today, someday. Listen to me. You need to learn to do all these things under stress without ceding control to the demon. It is the only way you will ever leave the Compound. Do you understand?"

I nodded. Understanding and doing were two distinctly different things, though.

"Good." Aleksei pulled a Glock from his shoulder holster and laid it on the hood of the van. "Since I'm feeling generous today…"

He stepped back and nodded at the closest soldier, who pulled the throwing knives strapped to his thigh off and laid them beside the gun. Our driver opened the passenger side door, reached under the seat, and pulled out a tire iron, adding it to the growing weapons pile. He also reached in his pocket and took out a handful of zip ties. He piled them next to the tire iron.

Aleksei gestured toward the van. "You can pick one—and only one—of these things to take with you."

I studied the selection. The gun I dismissed immediately. Whatever surprises Aleksei had in store for me inside that fort, I was positive a bullet wouldn't take it out. The throwing knives were tempting, but despite carrying around my own set for months, they'd never been useful for anything other than cutting thread while sewing. *Pass.* The tire iron was a definite contender. One good swing, and it could do some real damage. Plus, it could serve as a pry bar.

I looked back at the tunnel that was blocked off with coiled razor wire attached to either side of the entrance. I could use the zip ties to secure the wire together to make a hole big enough to climb through and avoid cutting my arms and face to shreds.

I bit my lip. One item. I needed to be smart about this.

Having witnessed some of Aleksei's more creative training techniques, I had no doubt there were surprises inside that were going to hurt like a bitch. But barring fire, decapitation, or falling into a vat of acid, nothing in that fort was going to kill me, thanks to the demon now bonded to me.

"Kali," Aleksei warned, tapping his overpriced Rolex. "You've got an hour to get through the course. Choose."

I stared at the opening again and thought about what was likely waiting for me inside. *One hour is a long time in Aleksei's world.*

I looked at the soldier who had donated his throwing knives to the cause. His name was Quinton, and he was one of Aleksei's favorites. While the others watched me with growing interest, Quinton's face remained impassive. He stood apart from the others, looking more like a biker than an assassin. Quinton wasn't the biggest guy here, but I knew beneath the scruffy beard and heavy leather jacket, his body was honed into a lethal weapon. I'd watched him training the elite soldiers at the Compound enough to know that, with the exception of Aleksei, he was the most dangerous man standing.

"Anything?" I asked, stepping closer to Quinton. His only reaction was the barest twitch of his lips.

Aleksei shook his head. "Any object, *ptichka*," he said. "Not a person."

"Fine," I agreed. I kept my gaze on Quinton and held my hand out. "Your jacket, please."

Everyone but Quinton laughed. Quinton studied me for a second before shrugging off his jacket and handing it to me without a word. He crossed his arms over his chest and waited to see what I'd do with it.

One of the other soldiers shook his head, still laughing at my expense. "Getting cold is going to be the least of your worries in there."

I ignored him and headed for the tunnel. Aleksei's hand shot out as I passed him.

He nodded at the jacket slung over my arm. "You sure that's what you want?"

I tipped my chin up. "I'm sure."

Aleksei frowned but let me pass.

When I reached the entrance, I took a minute to study the razor wire. It was attached securely with long metal spikes. If I drew on the demon's strength, I could probably pull them out, but the razor wire wound around each spike would shred my palms. Fortunately, that wasn't my only option.

By now, Aleksei and the rest of the soldiers had moved close enough to watch the show. Only his witch hung back, chanting in the background. *One worry at a time*, I told myself. I shot them all an irritated glance, but it did nothing to dissuade them from crowding in behind me.

I had no idea what awaited me in that abandoned tunnel. If the last year had taught me anything, it was not to rush in half-cocked. I needed to prepare as best I could before facing off with Aleksei's little horrorscape.

I sat on the ground and untied my boots before tugging

them off. I ignored the soldiers' running commentary about my odds. Boots in hand, I used the razor wire to saw through both ends of each of my shoelaces, careful not to take too much. Shoelaces should work just as well as zip ties to tie back razor wire.

I pulled my boots back on, tying a simple knot in each to keep them on my feet. I'd happily cut them off and pitch them in the trash when this was all over. The peanut gallery quieted. Aleksei nodded at me in approval as he caught on.

Next, I folded one of the jacket sleeves in half. Using the razor wire, I sliced a hole the size of my middle finger above the cuff before repeating it on the other sleeve. I heard Quinton curse behind me, but I ignored him as I zipped myself into his jacket. Even though I was swimming in it, the thick leather would offer a modicum of protection against the razor wire. I threaded my middle fingers through the holes I made so the sleeves covered my palms.

Armed with four modest lengths of shoelace, I looked around the area until I found a sturdy stick. I half-expected Aleksei to reiterate his one-item rule and snatch the stick away, but he didn't object. I'd take my small wins where I could get them. After placing one of the severed shoelace ends between my teeth, I tucked the rest in my pants pocket. Cargo pants might be ugly as sin, but at least they had a lot of pockets.

The stick was just wide enough to wedge between two of the sharp lengths of razor on the wire, which proved helpful as I used the stick to pull the wire toward the wall of the entrance. When I had the wire as taut as I could get it, I held the pressure on the stick with my left hand while awkwardly tying the wire to the nearest coil with the other. One-handed tying turned out to be more challenging than I'd anticipated.

It took me several tries to get the wire secure. I stood back to admire my handiwork. I'd managed to widen the opening until it was big enough to step through. Barely.

Because Quinton's jacket was so big on me, I could pull it over my head while still keeping my body covered. Even though I took my time going through the wire, I still managed to snag my left pant leg. The razor wire sliced fabric and skin, leaving a bead of my blood behind. *Can I still get tetanus?* I wondered. *Or is hosting a demon as good as an updated vaccination? Guess I'll find out.*

At least the jacket had done its job and protected my face. Unwilling to leave it behind, I slid it off my head. *You never know when a well-constructed leather jacket will come in handy,* I thought smugly.

"Getting in was the easy part," Aleksei called from the other side of the entrance. "Getting out in one piece is going to be harder."

Of course, it would. I gave my eyes a moment to adjust before making my way deeper into the unknown.

CHAPTER 6

t first, I assumed the eyes watching me from the dark belonged to werewolves. Despite knowing several werewolves, the only one I'd seen in wolf form had been Ruby. She'd seemed massive, but since she'd been trying to kill me at the time, my perception might have been skewed. I squinted at the dark shapes in the tunnel, trying to make out their sizes.

I counted four sets of eyes, all of them intent on me as I made my way deeper into the tunnel. I braced myself for attack, but they made no move toward me. As I cautiously inched closer, I could see they weren't werewolves at all but rather stray dogs that must have sought shelter in the abandoned tunnels. Three of the dogs were large, but they were skittish as they huddled next to the wall. The fourth dog was a tiny Chihuahua who stood in front of the other three, teeth bared.

"It's okay. I'm not going to hurt you," I said, keeping my voice soft and my movements deliberate.

On a different day, I would have taken as much time as

needed to reassure them that not all humans were assholes, but I couldn't afford the time it would take to win them over. The best I could do was offer them a few words of encouragement and the half-eaten granola bar I'd stuffed in my pants pocket. I broke it into pieces in my palm. Even with the promise of food, the dogs eyed me cautiously.

"Here you go, puppers." I scattered the chunks, leaving some distance between them to avoid fighting. After rewrapping the last little bit, I tucked it back into my pocket for later.

I crossed to the opposite side of the tunnel, heartened when I saw one of the dogs—a scruffy German Shepherd mix —nosing the granola bar in interest. He looked up at me with grateful eyes before going back to the food. The others watched me warily, and my heart broke as much for whatever put that look in their eyes as it did for their matted fur and tucked tails. Unlike the big dogs, the Chihuahua ignored the food to snarl and lunge at me whenever I got too close.

I like this one, Raum announced. *He's like a demon in rat form. We should keep him.*

I wanted to save them all, but I had to keep moving. I kept my gait steady as I passed them, pausing long enough to toe a granola bar chunk closer to the Chihuahua.

"I'll come back for you," I whispered, even though I wasn't sure it was a promise I could keep.

The further I ventured into the tunnel, the darker it got. Without a cell phone to light the way, I'd soon be forced to glide my hand along the wall and fumble around in the dark. That didn't bode well for me making it out of here unscathed. Aleksei's directive to draw on the demon's enhanced senses echoed in my head. In terms of demon powers, borrowing Raum's enhanced sight seemed about as innocuous as I was going to get.

I waited until I was a fair distance away from the dogs before stopping. I might feel sorry for them, but I wasn't stupid enough to turn my back on a pack of scared and starving animals who knew I had food.

I leaned against the wall of the tunnel, welcoming the chill that saturated my clothes. It gave me something to concentrate on, and I could use all the grounding I could get. Closing my eyes, I ran my fingertips over my tattoo and concentrated on the bond. Each time I reached for the demon, it got easier—more instinctual. I tried not to think too much about that fact.

Raum stirred but didn't speak. Although I'd drawn on the demon's sight before, it had been channeled through the crow. This time, I pinned the crow to my skin and took just enough power that my own vision sharpened. Within seconds, I could see as well in the dark as I had outside the tunnel. Along with my new night vision, my confidence grew. I'd drawn on the link and remained firmly in control.

I was deep underground when Aleksei sprung his trap. Because I was expecting an ambush, I had psyched myself up to fight. But he didn't send his soldiers in after me. He didn't have to. The deep rumble from the first explosion came only seconds before the tunnel began collapsing in front of me. I pivoted, intending to sprint for the entrance I'd come in through. I wasn't fast enough. A second explosion closed off my only exit before I'd taken half a dozen steps in that direction.

I dropped to the ground and covered my head with my arms, expecting the ceiling to come down on me next. Aleksei's team was too skilled at explosives for that. When the dust settled, I found myself exactly where he had intended: buried in a stone cell of his making.

"Asshole!" Not even shifter hearing was strong enough to catch my insult through several feet of rubble, but I screamed at him anyway.

I told you to kill that one, Raum said.

I didn't have time to wallow in self-pity or argue with a demon, so instead, I got to work. Grabbing the smallest chunks of debris, I began piling them next to the tunnel walls. I chose to dig my way further into the tunnel, knowing Aleksei would just send me back inside if I made my way back to him.

"Asshole," I yelled again as one of my fingernails caught on a jagged edge and ripped off to the quick.

The angrier I got, the harder the demon bond pulsed, Raum's commentary running through my head. *You are too weak on your own. Give me the reins, and we'll be out of here in no time.*

I ignored him and took a couple deep breaths to calm down. It didn't take long to stack all the smaller chunks neatly along the wall. What was left was a giant piece that probably weighed several hundred pounds. On a good day, I could heft a hundred pounds or so. There was no way I was getting out of here on my own.

Fine, I told Raum. *Together.*

He hummed his approval. It faded when I sat down cross-legged in the middle of the tunnel like I would in some high-end yoga studio.

You'll never clear that debris sitting on your ass, girl, Raum mocked.

Shut up! I snapped. *I'm trying to calm my mind.*

Your mind isn't going to get you out of this mess. You need muscle for that, he quipped.

I ignored him, and eventually he quieted, waiting to see

what I'd do. It only took a few minutes to slow my heart rate and breathing enough that I felt back in control. Gradually, I opened the bond until Raum's energy hummed through my veins. The rush was incredible.

The ache in my lower back from stacking rubble disappeared. I watched the cut on my leg from the razor wire knit itself back together again until the skin was smooth and unmarked. Raum's strength flowed into me until I felt invincible. The urge to open myself completely to the bond rose before I dialed it back to a manageable level.

"I'm in control," I said as much to myself as to Raum.

Sure, you are.

I made quick work of the rest of the debris, lifting the giant chunk of fallen rock as easily as I would a bolt of cloth. This time, I didn't bother shutting myself off from the bond again. Whatever Aleksei had in store for me next, I needed to be ready. I focused on my crow tattoo until it unfurled its wings and flew ahead to scout for me. I let the crow's vision guide me, jogging after it for quite a while before the tunnel opened into an underground room with two more tunnels veering off from it.

I paused, listening at the mouth of each tunnel. The one on the right was devoid of sound, but I caught a slow drip of water from the tunnel on the left. Listening more intently, I heard something that made my blood run cold—a voice I'd recognize no matter how faint. It was Riley, and she sounded afraid as she yelled for someone to let her out. I broke into a run.

After the confines of the tunnel, the room it opened into seemed cavernous. Judging by the munitions boxes stacked on the floor, it was probably the basement of one of the forts Aleksei mentioned. I made my way toward the set of dark stairs centering the far wall, pausing to listen before making my ascent. I could no longer hear Riley, but the sound of water was now more of a rush than a drip. I took the stairs two at a time, sending the crow ahead of me once more.

I stumbled, cracking my knee against a stone step, but the pain barely registered. The stairs opened into ruins. Three walls remained, and part of a fourth wall looked as if someone had blasted their way through it. Broken bottles and trash littered the space. My crow was perched on an opening in the far wall that, at one time, must have been a window.

I directed him toward a grate on the floor. As he peered down through the grate, his eyesight allowed me to see the top of Riley's head in high-definition color, along with the dark water rising around her. I called the crow back to me and let my rage draw more of the demon's power into me as I cleared the stairs and skidded to a halt. I dropped to my knees on the wet floor next to the grate and looked down. Riley was trapped in a five-by-five-foot cell. Unfortunately, she was also at least twenty feet below me.

"Riley," I yelled down at her. "Hold tight. I'm going to get you out of there."

She looked up, her vivid blue eyes glowing in the darkness. "Hurry," she called. The water was waist-level and rising rapidly.

I drew strength from the bond and grabbed the metal with a hand, prepared to yank it free. It wasn't until the electric current hit, seizing my muscles and stealing my breath, that I saw the thin wire attached to one corner. It took several terrifying seconds to pry my hands loose.

I lay on my side where I fell, my cheek pressed against the wet stone. If I hadn't had the demon to draw on, I wouldn't have been able to get free.

You're welcome. Raum sounded smug.

"Kali?" Riley's voice brought me back to the present.

I forced myself to a sitting position and rolled my neck to work out some of the tight muscles. When I stood, I staggered on my feet. I tugged harder on the bond until I felt steady again. Walking to the wall, I grabbed the wire running alongside it and yanked it free of the grate. I leaned over to check the water level—chest high. "Hang on."

This time, the grate came free, and I tossed it across the room. I lay down on my stomach and gauged the size of the hole in the floor. It was wide enough to climb through, but it would be a snug fit. I looked around the room for something I could use to pull Riley up through the opening, but there was nothing long enough.

I leaned my head through the opening. "Try to brace your legs against one wall and your back against the other. Then use your legs to inch up the wall. Once you're close enough, I can grab you and pull you out."

"I can't. My foot is secured to the floor."

I swore under my breath. If I didn't do something fast, Riley was going to drown.

"You need to shift, then." In goat form, her leg would be small enough to get loose. "Once your leg is free, you can shift back and climb out."

Riley tilted her head to look up at me. "I can't shift."

The image of the dark-haired witch chanting flashed in my head, and I cursed. She must have been doing some kind of spell that prevented shifting.

With the water lapping against Riley's collarbone, I didn't have time to waste on conversation. I took off the leather jacket and lowered myself into the hole feet first. "Scoot as far to the side as you can," I told her.

When she complied, I dropped into the water. I let the weight of my boots and clothes drag me down, holding my breath as I went under. I found the chain wrapped around Riley's left leg and yanked it from the floor. Then I ducked underneath her until her legs were on my shoulders, and I started climbing.

Even drawing on the demon, my lungs were burning and my legs shaking by the time my head surfaced above the water. I waited for Riley to brace her arms on either side of the opening and hoist herself out. Once she was free, she shook the water from her hair but made no move to help me out. It was so unlike her that I wondered if she was in shock.

From the tidbits she'd shared about her life before coming to Kansas City, I knew she'd weathered more than her share of bad situations. I just hoped Aleksei's stunt hadn't forced her to relive something she'd rather have left buried in her past.

After pulling myself through the opening, I did a visual inventory of the room, looking for additional threats. Seeing none, I grabbed Quinton's jacket and put it on before turning back to Riley. "Are you okay?"

"I didn't think you'd get me out in time." Her voice was surprisingly steady, as if making a detached observation about someone else.

"I'm sorry you got roped into all of this." I frowned. How had she gotten pulled into this? Had Aleksei taken her weeks ago in preparation for this? "How long have you been here?"

"In the hole?" she asked.

"No. How long have you been in Romania?"

Riley shrugged. "It doesn't matter."

Before I had time to question her further, one of Aleksei's soldiers ducked his head into the opening in the wall. "Time's up," he said. "Get your asses outside." And then he was gone again.

Riley followed without complaint, leaving me standing alone, wondering what the hell was going on. *Why is she cooperating? Is she part of this?*

By the time I crawled out of the old fort, everyone had cleared out. Fortunately, it wasn't hard to see which way they'd gone. The trampled vegetation made a clear path that I followed to the waiting group. Everyone except the witch and the driver was there when I stumbled out of the underbrush looking like a drowned rat.

Quinton's eyes narrowed when he saw the state of his jacket, but he didn't say anything. Everyone else carried on their jovial conversations like they hadn't just risked a woman's life for a stupid training exercise.

Riley was standing next to the big vamp, who was coiling the wire attached to the generator he'd used to electrify the metal grate. My fingers twitched with the need to twist his head from his fat neck, but I forced myself to keep walking. He was second on my shit list at the moment, and I was headed straight for the top.

I stopped in front of Aleksei. "You could have killed her," I snarled.

Aleksei barely spared me a glance. "She was never in real danger."

Even though I launched myself at him without warning, Aleksei met me halfway. He wrapped one arm around my neck as he twisted his body to the side, effectively pinning me in a headlock. "That's enough."

Not even close. I was playing with fire, but I was too angry to care as I pulled more power from Raum. "Let me go!" I infused my words with the demon's power to compel, and Aleksei dropped his arm from my neck.

Once I was free of Aleksei's hold, I drove my fist into his gut with enough force that his feet left the ground. I spun away from him and dropped into a fighter's stance, demon-fueled rage coursing through my body.

Yesssss, Raum cheered. *We should pull his beating heart from his body and eat it.*

I stumbled. *Gross!*

"Kali, stop," Aleksei said.

"Look at her eyes," Riley hissed.

"Oh shit." But it was too late to pull back. My eyesight went hazy, and I slumped to the ground, caught in another of Raum's visions.

The warehouse I found myself in wasn't one I recognized, but the scene playing out inside it was sickening in its familiarity. A summoning circle was spray-painted in red on the floor, and a body was immobilized inside its boundary. Unlike the witches whose deaths I had helped investigate, the man inside this circle was held down with chains fastened to metal rings secured to the floor. His limbs were stretched tight enough there was no room for movement. Still, his muscles bunched and pulled, trying to rip free from the chains that bound him.

I committed the scene to memory, cataloguing every detail I could. But I wasn't the one in the driver's seat for this vision, so I couldn't move my head to get the three-hundred-and-sixty-degree view I wanted. From my vantage point, I had a clear view of the man. He was in his prime, and he had a lean body and a face that held a hint of youth. The man's eyes were open and fixed on a point beyond my line of sight. For a long time, nothing changed. The wait was excruciating. I was as powerless as the man bound in the circle. Only the clenching of the man's fists warned me that someone was coming.

I expected the person who'd orchestrated this scene to be dressed in some kind of pretentious ceremonial robe, not faded blue jeans and a rumpled Pantera t-shirt. But then again, Frederick Masterson had never looked scary. He appeared unassuming—nerdy even—which was how he had once lured me in with nothing more than a shy smile and awkward overtures of friendship. Masterson was the kind of evil I never saw coming. By the time the demon he housed finally showed himself, I'd been blindsided.

Now, as he approached the man bound in the summoning circle, Masterson's lips were pursed as if whistling a tune I couldn't hear. If there were others in the room with him, I couldn't see them. All I could see was Masterson leaning closer to his victim, ripping open the man's shirt, and carving a demon mark into his chest. The vision flickered like an old television set, and I woke to blackness.

CHAPTER 7

Raum receded, taking the blackness with him. I was sprawled in the dirt, clumps of grass matted to my still-wet hair. The big vamp was crouched on his haunches next to me, staring intently into my eyes. It was more than a little unsettling.

He turned to Aleksei, who stood nearby. "She's back."

Aleksei stepped closer but didn't bend down to check on me. Given that I'd just attacked him, it was a wise choice on his part. I awkwardly sat up. When I spotted Riley, I searched her face to make sure she was okay. Something shifted there, making me clutch my head as I stared at her. She noticed me studying her—piecing it together—and took a hasty step back.

"Are you fucking kidding me?"

She looked to Aleksei for direction, but I wasn't ready to be dismissed. I put the full demon in my next command. "Drop the spell."

As I watched, her features blurred and settled back into the face of the witch from earlier. I glared as her hair quickly faded from bright pink to dark brown, her eyes turning wary and moss colored. "A distortion spell," I muttered, clenching my fists at my sides. If the vision hadn't left me so drained, I would have attacked Aleksei all over again for his manipulation.

Aleksei gestured for the witch to leave, as if losing sight of her would somehow lessen my rage at the stunt. Before I could let loose the string of profanities on the tip of my tongue, Aleksei reached down and yanked me to my feet. He held on until I was steady, then smartly took a step away from me. He made no apology, though. "Tell me about the vision," he ordered.

I clamped my jaw shut and stared at a tree behind him, silently counting to ten. When it did nothing to reduce my anger, I counted again.

Aleksei waited until I had it under control before prodding me. "The vision?"

Through gritted teeth, I told him about the vision. "I need to get word to Craig."

Aleksei frowned. "We don't even know when this vision happens. It could be something that occurred years ago."

I considered that possibility and dismissed it out of hand. If Raum were showing me an old crime, Craig would have uncovered it a month ago when we were investigating the witch murders. The similarities with the circle and Masterson performing his demon summoning ritual were uncanny. No way would Craig have missed the connection when he was digging into similar supernatural disappearances that could've helped us hunt down the killer.

"I don't think so. Craig would have pieced it together already if that were the case. I think these are things that have either happened recently—while I've been here at the Compound—or are about to happen."

Aleksei didn't look convinced. "Even if you're right, it could be anywhere in the world. What makes you think it has anything to do with Kansas City?"

I bit my lip. "Maybe it's doesn't. But it's connected to Frederick Masterson, and that makes it connected to me." I looked at Aleksei's pocket where his cell phone was vibrating. "Are you going to get that?"

"Describe the man again," he demanded instead of answering it.

A few seconds later, the phone vibrated again, saving me from recounting the vision for the third time. Aleksei pulled out his phone and checked the number before answering curtly. "Ward."

I clambered closer at Craig's name, glaring at faux-Riley, who was smart enough to keep her distance. Hopefully, Craig was about to reassure me that real Riley was safe and sound in Kansas City. I held my hand out expectantly for Aleksei to give me the phone. Instead, he put Craig on speaker.

"She's here but make it quick. We need to get back to the Compound." Aleksei's tone was clipped.

"I'm here, but I need to tell you about my latest vision." Although I was eager for word about Riley, I led with the vision. I hit the high points for Craig, describing the man in the vision as well as I could from memory. Based on the heavy chains securing him, we agreed that the man was likely a shifter. "He's building his army, then."

"It looks that way," Craig said. "I'll ask around to see if anyone matching your description has gone missing recently."

"Thanks. And Riley? Is she okay?"

"I think so," Craig said.

That wasn't exactly a ringing endorsement. "What do you mean?"

"She wasn't at her apartment when I went to check."

I was quiet as my mind worked overtime with all the possible things that could have happened to her.

Craig interrupted my worryfest. "When I didn't find her, I went to see the witches."

Aleksei raised an eyebrow but didn't say anything.

"And?" I asked.

"They assured me that Riley is fine, but they refused to tell me where she is." He let out a frustrated breath. "They'll only talk to you."

I relaxed a little. "Are they there now?"

"They are."

"Okay, put them on the line."

"That's not going to work," Craig said.

Aleksei began to pace, losing what little patience he had.

I trailed after Aleksei, who still held the phone in his hand. "Why not?"

"They're demanding a video call."

Aleksei's eyebrows shot up. "You're telling me you're not able to handle some local witches?"

"Not these witches," Craig grumbled.

Aleksei scowled at the phone as if Craig could see him. Aleksei rolled up his shirt sleeves. "We've got more important things to worry about, here. Put the witches on, and I'll handle them."

I heard shuffling in the background, and then Helen's voice came on. "Who is this?" She adopted her usual imperious tone.

"Aleksei Volkov."

"Volkov?" she asked.

His shoulders went back, and he looked pleased at the

sudden uncertainty in her voice. "You've heard of me, then. Good."

"You?" Helen scoffed. "No. But are you related to Max Volkov?"

He sidestepped her question. "I'm the Volkov in charge of the Compound." Aleksei and Max had more than a healthy dose of sibling rivalry between them, and it was clear he didn't like to be lumped under his older brother's umbrella.

Helen chuckled. "Ah, you're the alpha's baby brother?"

I pressed my lips together to repress my smile. The conversations around us stopped, all of Aleksei's soldiers suddenly more interested in our phone call than each other.

Aleksei stood momentarily speechless as he stared at his phone. Finally, he bared his teeth, all veneer of civilization peeled away to give me a glimpse of the predator beneath the fancy suits and stylish haircut. "Get on with it, witch," he demanded.

I choked, already knowing how that was going to go down.

Someone gasped on the other end of the line, and there was a minute of tense silence. "Well, someone is too big for his britches," Alyce piped up in the background.

Helen was less flippant about Aleksei's posturing. "What did you say to me, you mangy little runt?" Helen didn't give him a chance to answer before launching into her tirade. "If you think you can intimidate me, you've got another thing coming, boy-o. I've got age spots older than you. Now, stop wasting my time and set up that video call."

I jumped in before Aleksei crushed the cheap flip phone he was white knuckling. "Helen, it's Kali. We don't have video on this cell phone. Can't you just tell me where Riley is?"

"Sorry, honey, but I'm going to need video before I share

that information," Helen said.

Aleksei ground his teeth. "I don't have time for this nonsense. Kali's here now. Tell her what you know, witch."

"We're going to need proof of life first," she said flatly. Alyce, Janis, and Bea all murmured their agreement.

"What the fuck are you talking about?" Aleksei growled. "This isn't a kidnapping."

"So you say," Helen countered.

He turned to me. "Tell her."

I cleared my throat. "Helen, I'm here of my own free will."

She harrumphed. "That sounds exactly like what someone in a hostage situation would say."

Aleksei stared down at the phone in his hand, at a loss for words.

"V-i-d-e-o," Helen drawled like she suspected he had trouble following simple instructions. "You've got one hour." She hung up.

I grabbed the phone out of his hand, clicked it off, and shoved it in his pocket. "Yeah, I'm gonna need that video call."

Aleksei grumbled under his breath. "Fine." He pointed at the van.

"One sec," I said, shrugging out of the leather jacket. "I'll be right back."

I ran back to the tunnel, where four sets of hopeful eyes stared out at me from the darkness. Afraid to startle them, I moved slowly, keeping my palms up to show I didn't mean any harm. I cooed sweet words as I reached in my pocket, taking out the last of my granola bar. The Chihuahua bared his teeth in a growl as I approached.

"Who's my brave boy?" I said as I neared him. I put a piece of the granola bar on the ground and waited. As soon as he went for it, I scooped him up and wrapped him in the leather jacket. After a few more half-hearted growls, he settled into my arms to nibble on his newfound treat.

"Come on, fellas," I coaxed, crumpling the rest of the granola bar and leaving a crumb trail for them to follow.

When Aleksei caught sight of my entourage, he tensed. "No fucking way!"

I ignored him and loaded all four dogs into the open van. Aleksei ranted while everyone else looked between the two of us. "You owe me," I countered, adjusting the dog in my arms. I climbed in and poked my head back out to look at Aleksei. He was still standing where I left him, looking shell-shocked. I motioned him to hurry up. "Come on! Helen isn't going to give us an extension."

Aleksei ignored the sidelong looks his soldiers were sending his way and climbed in the back of the van. He handed me the hood and rapped on the door once it slid shut. "Let's go."

"Here." I thrust the leather-wrapped bundle into his arms.

He took it before he realized it wasn't just a jacket. He looked at the mangy Chihuahua and grimaced. When he reached for the jacket to cover the dog again, the Chihuahua bared his teeth at Aleksei. "Stop that," Aleksei ordered, letting his wolf rise to the surface. The little guy took one look at Aleksei's eyes and promptly sank his teeth into his hand.

Raum hummed in approval. *We should name him Raum.*

We are not naming the dog after you.

He huffed but settled back into silence. With one last growl, the little dog released his bite. Then, he curled up in Aleksei's lap and promptly fell asleep. Before Aleksei could hand him back to me, I pulled the hood over my head and leaned back. After a few minutes, I started humming *Who Let the Dogs Out* and thought of Riley.

Liv was waiting for us when we arrived back at the Compound. When I told her what was going on, she smirked at Aleksei and opened her mouth.

Aleksei held up a warning finger. "Don't start."

Because the courtyard proved overwhelming for our strays, we got the dogs settled in Aleksei's office with food, water, and a vamp babysitter. The Chihuahua whined when Aleksei put him on the floor with the others. With a glare in my direction, he picked the little guy back up and made him a bed on his executive chair. "Let's go."

I smiled. I guess even assassins had a soft spot for little dogs.

"Move your ass," he snapped when I hesitated. "I don't have all day."

I hustled after him, with Liv close on my heels. Once we were through the doors, Liv elbowed me in the side and mouthed, "Helen?"

I nodded and bit my lip at the look of pity she leveled at his stiff back.

The communications room had an entire wall of computers monitored by the tech guy Liv had put in a choke-hold. He didn't look happy to see us. Along the opposite wall was a giant screen with a projector aimed at it.

"Two minutes. Connect the call," Aleksei ordered.

Little Mr. Sunshine bustled around the room searching for something. He shot Liv a dirty look when she hopped up on one of the computer tables. "Why do you need to be here?" He reached around her and righted the computer monitor she'd bumped into. "You should leave."

Liv grinned at him and tucked her feet underneath her until she was sitting cross-legged on his computer table. "I wouldn't miss this for the world."

Aleksei pointed at Liv. "Stay off camera."

She nodded, instantly sobering. "I know."

The fact that he was letting her stick around with a mere warning to stay off camera was surprising, given how ferociously he guarded the Compound's secrecy. Liv had spent several months around Helen while on assignment to watch me in Kansas City. Liv—or Olivia as I'd known her then—had stayed with her aunt Janis, who was one of Helen's closest friends. And where Helen went, the other witches followed, so there was zero chance they wouldn't all be on the video call.

Liv pulled a balaclava from her back pocket and put it on, tucking errant strands of her distinctive hair beneath it. Both Liv and Janis were redheads, but while Janis wore her hair long and henna-infused, Liv preferred her strawberry-blond hair short and sassy to match her attitude.

Aleksei checked his watch, his jaw tense. "Thirty seconds."

Computer guy scrambled until he came up with an oversized remote he aimed at the projector. He connected the video, and we all waited for Helen to pick up the call. It took several tries before the witches answered.

When the video feed finally clicked on, Janis was so close to the screen, I could see her chin hair. "Hello?" she yelled. "Who's there?" Janis leaned in and blinked into the camera lens like it was a peephole.

"You're too close to the camera," Helen told her, slapping her on the back of the head. "Back up!"

After a couple more blinks, Janis obliged. Once she stepped back, I could see all of Riley's witches. The four women ranged in age from early sixties to late seventies and —despite their current technological fumbling—were some of Kansas City's magical powerhouses. They were also the witches who had taken Riley under their wings when she moved to Kansas City as a teen runaway. If anyone knew where she was, it would be them.

Janis, Alyce, and Bea were all taller than the tiny four-foot-ten Helen, but Helen was the undisputed leader. At the moment, Helen was in the middle, arms crossed and eyes narrowed as she glared at Aleksei. "You're late."

Aleksei didn't waste time arguing. He inclined his head, opting for diplomacy over strong-arming. "My apologies." He gestured to me. "As you can see, Kali is unharmed and here of her own volition."

I stepped up next to Aleksei and waved. "Hi everyone! Aleksei's right. I'm here willingly."

Alyce elbowed Helen in the side, earning herself a slap to the arm. Alyce batted Helen's hand away then bent down and whispered something to her.

Helen nodded. "Kali, why don't you come a little closer, honey," she said.

I took a couple steps closer, but Helen wasn't satisfied. She motioned for me to come closer yet. Once I was standing in front of Aleksei, she smiled and nodded for me to stop.

"Now then." Helen stared intently into the camera. "Blink twice if he's holding you there against your will."

All four women leaned closer to examine my reaction. While she wasn't entirely off base, the last thing I needed was for Helen to decide I needed rescuing. Afraid she'd interpret normal blinking for some kind of distress signal, I held my eyelids wide open until my eyes started to water.

"Enough with the theatrics." Aleksei moved up next to me. He'd shed his suit jacket and had adopted his big-man-on-campus stance. *So much for diplomacy.* His legs were braced apart to take up space, his shoulders squared, and his arms crossed to show off what I liked to call stealth biceps. Aleksei only brought out the guns when he wanted a shortcut intimidation tactic. Clearly, he didn't understand these witches.

Bea bumped Helen with her hip as she moved in closer to the camera. "Hello there, tiger," Bea cooed. Today, Bea was wearing her favorite pair of booty-enhancing leggings and an off-the-shoulder cropped sweatshirt that had "OG Cougar in the House" spelled out in rhinestones.

"Wolf," he corrected. Apparently, Aleksei didn't appreciate being lumped in with the cats.

"Even better." Bea laughed. "I like a little growl in my men." She bared her teeth and rumbled a growl.

I glanced at Aleksei, who had now dropped his arms to his side. I guess he didn't have a comeback for that. Liv laughed before clapping a hand over her mouth.

"Who's that?" Helen asked suspiciously.

Aleksei recovered. "It's not important. Let's get on with it."

"Fine," Helen said.

"Fine," Aleksei agreed.

I broke in before things deteriorated further. "Helen, I need to know Riley is okay."

Helen's expression softened. "Riley is fine, dear."

"Where is she?"

Helen and Alyce shared a look, but I didn't know what it meant. "She's on a job," Helen said finally.

I narrowed my eyes. "What kind of job?"

Bea winked at me. "Acquisitions."

I groaned. "What is she stealing?"

Helen shrugged. "She didn't say. All I know is that she said she'd be out of town for four or five days."

"And that was when?"

Helen shifted her weight and looked at the ground. "Four days ago."

"I'm sure Riley will be back any time now," Alyce assured me, her dark eyes earnest.

Riley was notoriously optimistic when it came to estimating the amount of time or difficulty for most tasks. If she said it would take four or five days, it probably meant five or six.

"And you don't know where she went?" I asked.

"No." Helen's lips thinned.

"What are you not telling me?"

Janis caved first. "Riley didn't seem like herself," she blurted, ignoring Helen's sharp look.

The low-level hum of anxiety that had begun in my gut when Helen first mentioned the job intensified. "How so?"

"She was so serious." Janis twisted the fabric of her skirt in her hands. "I've never seen Riley like that. It's like a switch flipped, and she went from our fun-loving girl to stone cold."

"You're exaggerating," Helen accused. "She was just focused, that's all."

Janis didn't contradict her, but the worry was still etched on her face.

I covered my eyes for a second, trying to figure out what could have caused a shift like that. A heavy hand dropped to my shoulder, and I didn't have to look up to know it was Aleksei's.

"Ward told me that Max is tracking your friend. He's the best tracker I know. He'll have her location pinned down in no time," Aleksei assured me.

All four women exchanged looks. "If our girl Riley doesn't want to be found, he's not going to find her." Helen glanced at me. "Sorry, hon. You'll just have to hold tight."

Aleksei bent closer to me while keeping the witches in his sights. "I guarantee he'll find her. There's no way your friend is going to elude my brother. He's tracked seasoned criminals. I hardly think he'll have trouble finding a slip of a girl."

Helen chortled and nudged Alyce in the ribs. "You hear that?" She shook her head. "Wolves and their damned egos."

Alyce stuck her hand down her top and rustled around in her bra until she came up with a wad of folded bills. "Twenty bucks says the alpha chases his tail until Riley decides to show up."

Janis, Bea, and Helen all shook their heads. "None of us are taking a bet that stupid," Helen said. She canted her chin toward the camera. "How about you, big man?"

Aleksei stiffened. "You're on, witch."

Am I the only one worried about her? "Back to the point," I said. "You'll tell Craig the second she's back?"

Helen met my eyes. "I'll tell Craig as soon as I hear from her. But try not to worry. That kid is tough as nails and wily as a coyote." She smirked at Aleksei as she said it.

Aleksei disconnected our call without responding. "You okay?" he asked me.

I stared at the blank screen. "I'll be okay when I know Riley is safe."

Aleksei looked at his watch. "Liv, why don't you and Kali get in some sparring practice."

Liv slid off the table without argument. "Sure thing, boss."

Aleksei didn't follow us out. Instead, he grabbed the remote from computer guy's hands and pointed to the door. "I need the room to make a call."

I left him to it, happy to throw on a pair of MMA gloves and work out my anxiety and aggression on the mat.

CHAPTER 8

In a place like the Compound, the only surprises were the ones orchestrated by the staff in the name of training. So, when a stranger dropped into the middle of the courtyard during sparring practice, it garnered attention. When the man in question was dressed in skinny jeans and a rumpled *Stranger Things* t-shirt with a katana sheathed at his waist, it drew a crowd.

I craned my neck to get a better look, but the mass of bodies between me and the show made it impossible to see. Liv was even shorter than I was, but unlike me, she wasn't above throwing a well-placed elbow to move the blockade. She grabbed my arm with one hand and used her other to clear our way. By the time we made it to the front, the Compound guards had the mystery man surrounded, forming a circle around him. They made no move to attack the man, but the tight circle was their not-so-subtle attempt at containment. I peered between two of the guards.

The man in the center appeared to be Japanese, with neatly cropped dark hair and an angular face. Despite being shorter

71

than most of the guards hulking around him, he would have looked deadly even without the sword. While the guards exchanged nervous glances and puffed up to take up more space, this man stood as still as a statue, his face blank. He stared at a point beyond the guards, his posture relaxed. I followed his gaze to determine what he was looking at.

Seeing where I was looking, Liv answered the unspoken question. "He's waiting for Aleksei." She nudged me and pointed to where the man's gaze was fixed. "Aleksei's office."

After several seconds of the standoff, one of the guards peeled away from the crowd and headed for the office. Aleksei opened his door before the guard reached it. Although they were too far away to make out their conversation, Aleksei scanned the crowd before the guard finished speaking. As soon as he caught sight of the mystery man, he stilled, eyes locked on the stranger. It was clear that Aleksei hadn't been expecting him. There was a charge in the air, a history between the two men that I couldn't decipher.

No one spoke, and after a few seconds, Aleksei bowed his head. "Kage Sato. Welcome."

At the mention of his name, there was a collective inhale. Immediately, the guards forming the circle broke ranks, dropping to one knee and bowing their heads.

Well, that was weird. I turned to Liv, who stood slack-jawed beside me. "Who is he?" I whispered.

She didn't answer.

Sato crossed to Aleksei, his only acknowledgement of the guards a slight incline of his head. He reached Aleksei, who stepped aside to fall in beside him. "This way."

When they were gone, Liv finally answered. "A legend."

From the looks on everyone else's faces, she wasn't exaggerating. "I'm gonna need you to be a bit more specific."

"Kage Sato is the first Shadow. His skills as an assassin are legendary, and his stealth as a spy unmatched." Liv's face was contorted into a mask of hero worship that made me uncomfortable. It reminded me too much of the time I went to Pentecostal church with a friend. It wasn't the snake handlers that had freaked me out. It was the awe on my friend's face as she reached for the serpent without a hint of self-preservation. I pinched Liv.

"Ow!" she yelled. "What did you do that for?"

"You're creeping me out."

She rubbed the spot I had pinched and glared at me, but at least she looked like herself again.

"So, why is he here?"

"Who?" Liv asked.

I rolled my eyes. "Sato."

"No idea." She tossed me a bo staff and grabbed one for herself. As everyone fell back into training mode, I threw myself into the motions while wondering if Sato's sudden appearance had anything to do with the visions I'd been having.

I didn't have to wait long to find out.

"Kali," Aleksei called. "In my office." He retreated back inside, not giving me a chance to answer.

I handed Liv my bo staff and headed for the open office door. Even leaning casually against the wall, Kage Sato's presence filled the room. There was something deeply unsettling about the level of stillness he maintained. It made me feel like I was under a microscope, and I fought the urge to squirm under the weight of his scrutiny.

Aleksei gestured to the two chairs in front of his desk. "Sit."

Sato moved to one of the chairs and stared down at it. A handful of kibble littered the seat. "What is that?"

When he spotted what had Sato's attention, Aleksei jerked his head toward me. I rolled my eyes but swept the dog food into my palm just the same. "Where is he?"

Sato frowned and glanced around the office.

I smirked. "He's under your desk, isn't he?"

Aleksei nodded curtly and held out his hand. I gave him the dog food, and he bent down to pile it on the floor under his desk. "Now, sit down," he ordered.

I sat next to Sato and waited for either of the men to tell me what was going on. Aleksei spoke first. "The Enclave has requested an audience to discuss your recent visions and evaluate your fitness. Kage will escort you."

Startled, I blinked at Aleksei. "In person?"

"Yes."

I frowned. "Fitness evaluation? Like some kind of iron man shit?" I looked down at my body, which had about as much muscle definition as it was going to get. I was in much better shape than I'd been a year ago, but the only six-pack I claimed was the beer Liv and I commandeered from the cafeteria refrigerator.

"Not that kind of fitness," Sato corrected. "They need to have assurances that allowing you to leave the Compound will not pose too large a danger."

"Too large," I repeated. "So, this is a risk versus reward determination?"

"Most decisions are," Sato agreed dispassionately.

I turned in my chair to find Sato watching me. "And after I meet with them? I'll be allowed to leave?"

We will leave either way, Raum insisted. Although I agreed with him, I kept that to myself.

"If the Enclave deems you fit to do so, yes. I will return you to the Compound unharmed, and Aleksei can make arrangements to see you home."

"When do we leave?" I asked, pretty sure the answer was now.

Sato didn't disappoint "Immediately."

"Pack for a week," Aleksei directed me, even though all of his attention remained on Sato.

"Two days," I countered. "And then I go home."

"Three days for the evaluation." Sato didn't look at me as he spoke.

"Deal," I said, like I had a choice in the matter. There was little point in pushing for answers I was certain neither man would give me, so I exited the room, leaving them to their stare down.

Liv was loitering outside the door. "What was that all about?"

Before I could answer her, Aleksei opened the office door. "That information is on a need-to-know basis."

"And I don't need to know." Liv's shoulders drooped. When Aleksei continued watching her, she threw up her hands. "Fine. I'm going." After sending one more assessing look my way, she slunk off in the opposite direction.

I managed to pack in ten minutes, which was a record for me. Based on Aleksei's irritated tapping when I returned, he wasn't as impressed by my hustle as I was. Although the two seemed to be past their standoff, Aleksei hardly looked happy to see us off. I wondered if he was worried about entrusting me to a notorious assassin, or if he was sad he hadn't been invited to the party. Odds were better for the latter. Either way, he didn't walk us out.

When we reached the training courtyard, I tilted my head

to look up. *Surely, he doesn't expect us to leave the same way he came in. Because climbing isn't really my forte.*

Sato noted where my attention was. "We'll leave through the front door." Although his face remained devoid of emotion, I swore I heard amusement in his tone.

The training courtyard was packed, and everyone stopped what they were doing to watch us leave. As soon as our backs were to the crowd, the murmur of voices kicked in. They may not have known where I was headed, but speculation about why Kage Sato was taking me out of the Compound was bound to make the rounds. The Compound might be built on secrecy, but those within its walls loved their gossip as much as anyone.

I wasn't sure what I expected a notorious assassin to drive, but it certainly wasn't the utilitarian gray Honda Accord. Once we were buckled in, Sato handed me a black silk blindfold that looked better suited to the bedroom than for travel to a clandestine meeting. I raised an eyebrow but took it.

"First lesson." Sato kept his eyes straight ahead, but I saw his lips twitch. "Use what you have."

I opened my mouth to ask why he had a bondage scarf, but when he turned to face me, all traces of humor were gone. He nodded at the scarf. I obediently tied it around my eyes and settled into the seat for the ride.

Unlike my previous escorts from the Compound, Sato didn't keep me in the dark for the entire trip. Twenty minutes in, he let me take off the blindfold. Despite trying several icebreakers, he wasn't a small talk kind of guy. After half an hour of unnerving silence, I cracked and turned on the radio to a Shakira song. Instead of shutting it off—or worse, turning it to an instrumental station like Aleksei would have—Sato's fingers tapped the beat on the steering wheel as he drove.

I relaxed into my seat and studied him. Now that he was lip-syncing "Whenever, Wherever," I had a harder time imagining him as a deadly assassin. Although it lent credibility to his spying prowess. Anyone who could shift gears this fast had to be an expert at blending in.

He drove straight for the coast—no bathroom breaks for him. I rolled down my window as we got closer, welcoming the cool breeze and listening to the sounds of the water. Sato parked at a small marina where several expensive yachts were docked. He grabbed my bag out of the trunk and tossed it to me.

"Stay close," he warned, handing his keys to a boy who couldn't have been a day over fourteen.

I glanced over my shoulder as the boy climbed into the car. He gave me a cheeky salute before backing out of the parking spot and speeding off.

I caught up to Sato. "Aren't you going to blindfold me again?"

He tilted his head and studied me. "Do you like to be blindfolded?"

Was he teasing me? With his blank expression, it was hard to tell. "No," I said. "I just thought—you know—" I widened my eyes. When he looked at me blankly, I cupped my hand around my mouth and whispered, "top secret."

Sato shook his head. "You're strange."

"I'm strange?" I sputtered. I scanned him from head to toe, pausing at the sword he wore openly.

"Yes." He picked up the pace, making his way down the line of exorbitantly expensive yachts without so much as glancing at them in appreciation.

I gawked. Having grown up in a neighborhood where living in the lap of luxury meant scoring box seats for the

Chicago Bulls, this kind of wealth warranted a little rubber-necking.

"You won't remember the route," Sato promised.

I tore my gaze from the sleek luxury boats I had been salivating over. "What do you mean, I won't remember?"

He kept walking, so I was talking to his back, but his voice carried over his shoulder. "Your memories will be altered, so you won't remember the trip to get to or from our destination. You'll only remember being there. Any details that could give away the location will be wiped."

I stopped abruptly. "I didn't agree to that."

Sato's laugh carried on the breeze, but he didn't slow down. "I didn't ask."

For a moment, I stood on the dock, glaring at his retreating back. I didn't like the thought of someone tampering with my memories. A wiry old man bumped into me. I barely felt the bag slide off my shoulder.

"Hey!" I shouted as the man sprinted away with my belongings. He was fast for an old guy. I turned to give chase, but Sato stopped me. I had no idea how he'd made it back to me so quickly, when he'd been so far away mere seconds ago.

He held my wrist in an iron grip, preventing me from giving chase. "Leave it," he commanded.

"But that's my stuff." I tried to yank my arm free.

"I told you to stay close." He pulled me along, only letting go of my wrist when I stopped struggling and trotted after him. "Let this be a lesson."

"A lesson not to trust little old men," I muttered.

"A lesson in obedience," he corrected.

I rolled my eyes but followed him. When we reached our ride, I stopped to stare. "Wicked."

In a line of shining, bone-white yachts, the sleek little

black number was drool worthy. Unlike the Accord, this baby was one hundred percent super-spy material. From a distance, the reflective slate surface would be virtually invisible against dark waters. It was like the stealth bomber of the seas, and it was freaking gorgeous. The lighter color of the decking contrasted beautifully with the dark exterior. The windows were heavily tinted and constructed of thick glass—bulletproof, without a doubt.

Sato reached a hand out and helped me climb onboard. A woman was already on deck, bustling to get the ship ready to sail. She was at least a decade older than me, with sun-kissed blonde hair and a generous sprinkle of freckles. She hummed a catchy tune while she worked, not pausing her preparations to greet us.

Sato did a quick sweep of the cabin while I waited awkwardly on deck. Since the biggest boat I'd been on was a pontoon rental in college that we'd filled with cheap beer and lake tunes, I didn't have the first clue about getting a yacht ready to sail.

It didn't take Sato long to inspect the small yacht.

"Where's the rest of the crew?" I asked when he joined us on the deck.

The woman laughed. "How many people do you think we need to sail a small boat?"

I shrugged because I had no idea.

She winked at me. "Don't worry. We know what we're doing." She tossed Sato a rope, and he set to work alongside her as if they'd done this dozens of times together. I wondered how often they made this trek to the super-secret Enclave headquarters.

"Make yourself comfortable." The woman gestured to the cabin. "The refrigerator is stocked."

She was friendly, but I recognized a dismissal when I heard one. I left them to their sailing preparations while I wandered the rest of the ship. The interior was even more stunning than the outside, all modern lines and high-end finishes. The immediate cabin was made up of a cream-colored leather seating area with a metal-edged glass table. A matching fully stocked bar divided the room from a pair of oversized captain's chairs with an expansive view of the Black Sea.

A short flight of stairs led below deck to the sleeping quarters. Inside, a large platform bed with a plush black comforter and dark gray pillows took up much of the room. The wall behind the bed was decorated with deep green wallpaper with close-set dark shimmering trees. A small desk, pocket closet doors, and a pair of stylish modern chairs completed the room.

Although the bedroom practically begged to be napped in, I made my way back up to the deck as I felt the boat set sail. I might not remember the trip to the Enclave, but that wasn't going to stop me from staying alert for the journey.

I rested my arms on the railing and soaked up the midday sun. It wasn't every day that a Midwestern girl like me had the opportunity to experience the Black Sea aboard a luxury yacht manned by notorious assassins. I was practically living the James Bond life. If Riley were here, she'd tell me all I needed was a sharp suit and some drop-dead gorgeous arm candy.

But Riley wasn't here. Despite the sunshine and blue waters, my mood was as dark as the demon stowed away inside me.

CHAPTER 9

Stepping off the yacht was like stepping into a different world. We were on a large island, and the otherwise still waters of the surrounding Black Sea churned near the rocky shoreline as if a storm were imminent. Sato left his helper to secure the boat while we made our way inland. We followed a well-worn path from the beach into the thick trees surrounding us. Before we made it more than a few hundred feet, a dense fog rolled in behind us, obscuring the shoreline and the yacht we'd arrived in.

"That's weird," I said.

The fact that Sato didn't have to look back to see what I was talking about told me it was a regular occurrence here. "Part of the island's defense," he confirmed.

We walked until there was no trace of the rocky beach, only thick masses of trees that crowded our path. I was so busy studying the flora and fauna around me that I careened into Sato's back when he stopped abruptly. Although his body tensed at the impact, he didn't complain. His heightened alertness made me uneasy.

I searched the area around us, but I didn't note any immediate dangers. "Why are we stopping?"

He held his palm out and ran it along an invisible surface. "The island wards are here. No one can get past them without me."

I wondered if that meant he'd set them. Until now, I'd have put money on him being some kind of shifter, based on the way he moved and his reputation for violence. But if he was the only one who could bypass these wards, either he was the witch who had set them, or he had some kind of magical key that allowed him to come and go despite the wards. He didn't look like a witch, but then again, there were a lot of people whose looks were deceiving in this world. I waited to see what he would do.

"You'll want to step aside for this." Sato wrapped his hand around my wrist and moved me off the path before turning his attention back to the wards.

I waited for him to orchestrate some combination of witchy hand gestures and incantations that would allow us to pass. He looked over his shoulder to make sure I was clear, then he formed an O with his lips and breathed a stream of frigid air across the wards that froze as it hit them.

I jumped back. "Ice!" I yelled stupidly, as if the man had no idea what was coming out of his mouth.

He chuckled. The ice crackled across the surface of the ward, lighting up symbols as if they were crystalized in the air. When the symbols faded, Sato stepped effortlessly through the ward and gestured for me to do the same. I held my hands out in front of me, testing the air as I walked. While the air was noticeably colder where he'd brought the wards down, it didn't harm me. I watched Sato as he repeated the process once I was through them, presumably erecting the wards once again.

"Are you a water elemental?"

He shot me an amused look. "Hardly."

I scrunched my face and tilted my head to look at him. "Then what?"

He ignored me and kept walking. Once we passed the wards, it didn't take long for us to reach our destination. The path opened to a clearing that held a sprawling building as well as several cottages and a few outbuildings of various sizes. The main building was white, with two wings that branched off a large two-story entrance lined with balconies. The front of the building had abundant windows framed by ornamental trees.

To the right of the building was a large glass greenhouse packed with garden plants. The wing on the left ended in an octagon, with floor-to-ceiling windows next to an Olympic-sized swimming pool. Both wings had rooftop solar panels and extended behind the building in a U-shape, hinting at an enclosed courtyard out back. Further away from the building were cottages tucked back into the trees. I was betting there were even more behind the main building, but it was blocking much of the view as we approached.

Sato observed my reactions as I took it all in. "Stunning, isn't it?"

"Yes," I agreed. It must have cost a fortune to build such an elaborate construction on an island like this. I wondered if there was some kind of supernatural dues or tax that I was supposed to be paying toward upkeep.

Sato allowed me a few minutes to bask in my first impressions before gesturing toward the front door. "It's time to seek answers."

I couldn't help but wonder if I was ready for the answers we were hunting. Something told me I would be walking out of here a different person than I walked in. Nonetheless, I squared my shoulders and followed him into the massive entryway.

Nerves fluttered in my stomach as I followed him through the entryway and into an opulent sitting room filled with antique upholstered furniture and expensive oil paintings. Sato moved to a gold cart laden with crystal decanters and expensive booze and turned to look at me. "You may want a drink for this."

My mouth watered at the thought of a double shot of high-end tequila, but I wasn't ready to dull what little instincts I had just to settle my nerves. I shook my head. "No thank you."

He shrugged. "Suit yourself." After pouring himself a glass of vodka, he crossed to the window, his back to me as he peered outside.

I cleared my throat. "Who exactly am I meeting with?"

He didn't turn around. "You'll be meeting with a representative."

"A representative?" I asked. "I thought I was here to meet with the Enclave."

Sato returned his empty glass to the cart. "No one meets with the entire Enclave."

"Except you?"

His lips twitched. "Except me."

I expected the Enclave representative to arrive momentarily. Despite the urgency of sending Sato to collect me, however, the Enclave member apparently wasn't in a hurry to meet with me. As the wait stretched out, I occupied myself by studying the oil paintings adorning the walls. Most of them were island landscapes with dark, moody waters and mythological sea creatures. I paused in front of the largest painting that depicted some kind of monster rising from the depths.

"A bit far from home for the Loch Ness monster," I said, leaning in for a better look.

Sato's choked laugh made me jump. Although I hadn't heard him move, he stood just behind me, arms crossed over his chest. "That's what you see?"

I shrugged. "What do you see?"

He stepped closer until our arms were almost touching. We stood side by side, examining the painting for several seconds like we were strangers admiring an art gallery exhibit. The more I looked at it, the more details I made out. Scales along its narrow body, a reptilian head rising from the waters like some kind of sea dragon.

"Well?" I prompted. "What is it that you see?"

"Loneliness." He sounded sad, but when I turned, he was already walking out. "I'll return in three days to take you back."

And with that, he was gone.

I was still scrutinizing the painting when I felt a presence at my back.

"I'm sorry to keep you waiting."

I didn't turn around immediately, the sudden pitch of my stomach holding me in place.

"Kali?" Her voice broke on my name, but I would recognize that voice anywhere.

My heart rate sped up, and the room shrank, but I couldn't bring myself to turn around. *It's a trick.* I nudged my shirt to the side to examine my tattoo, but it was as still as a picture. My body stiffened. "No," I whispered.

"Kali," she repeated. "I can explain."

Those three words broke me. Whatever came after them wouldn't matter. The only thing that mattered was what they meant—that her leaving me had been a choice.

I turned slowly, my eyes fixed on the ground. When I gathered the courage to raise them, my grandmother looked like a stranger. Her graying hair had gone full silver and grown long in her absence. She now wore it plaited over one shoulder. The laugh lines I remembered were still there, but her skin had become more luminous. Island life agreed with her. Her body had grown stronger, too, her arms defined and her calves below the hem of her skirt testament to physical activity. I swallowed past the lump forming in my throat and forced myself to meet her eyes.

Ever since I was a child, people had said I'd inherited her eyes, those deep brown pools that reflected everything she felt. As I looked into them now, I saw the emotions warring for dominance—grief and happiness, sorrow and guilt. From her reaction, I knew mine were the same.

She took a cautious step toward me, but I held up a hand. I took a shuddering breath. There were a million things I wanted to say to her, questions that had kept me awake in the middle of the night, but only one mattered. "Why?"

"Kali, please, sit. I'll answer all of your questions, but the answers aren't easy."

I clenched my fists at my sides, ignoring her offer of a comfortable chair. I eyed the cart of alcohol, though. *If there was ever a time that warranted a shot of tequila, this is definitely it.* Without comment, she crossed the room and poured us both a drink, handing me mine before tossing hers back with a grimace. I drank it and poured myself a second.

"I need to know why you did this." I looked at her. "Why would you fake your own death?"

Her hand trembled as she took my glass from me and put it back on the cart. She sat on the edge of a loveseat patterned with faded tropical birds. "I want you to understand, when I came to Romania, I didn't know this would happen."

I looked away.

"You got the letter I left for you?"

"I did."

"So, you know I came to Romania to find the man who had been following you and Claire?"

My throat tightened at the mention of my twin, but I nodded. Although I hadn't found the letter until several months ago, Grandma Dottie had left it for me in the glove compartment of my Volkswagen Beetle—a college graduation gift from her. In the letter, she'd told me that I, like her, was a necromancer. She'd also told me about the man who had shown up outside our house and later at Claire's funeral. She'd followed his trail to Romania in search of answers, much as I had done a short time ago. In my case, the trail had led me to Garadin Aldea, the vampire who had killed my sister Claire all those years ago.

"I killed him," I said, no remorse in my voice. I met her eyes. "I lit him on fire, and I watched him burn for what he did to her." I took a deep breath. "What I thought he did to you."

She closed her eyes and swayed in her seat. "I know."

The demon mark flared to life, feeding on the unbridled rage that coursed through me whenever I thought of Claire's killer. I may have succeeded in avenging her death, but it had done little to extinguish the anger at the senselessness of her loss. I ran a hand over the crow undulating against my chest.

Grandma Dottie watched my movements, her mouth

tightening as she looked at Raum's mark on my skin. I lifted my chin. "I don't regret killing him."

She looked up, her eyes fierce. "Good."

We sat in silence for a few minutes, searching for what to say next. *How do you get past the years of grief? What do you say to someone you thought dead and buried?* At least the mystery of why I had been unable to summon her spirit was solved.

Grandma Dottie cleared her throat. "When I arrived in Romania, I followed Aldea to Wallace Ratcliff's home." She gauged my reaction.

"I found the photos." The photos showed both Ratcliff and Aldea in the master vampire's home.

Grandma Dottie smiled. "I heard you broke into the safe deposit rental place to retrieve them."

"I had help." The reminder of Riley spiked my anxiety at her absence. *One thing at a time, Kali. When I get back to the Compound, there will probably be a message from Craig telling me all about the trouble she got up to without me. Riley is strong and smart, and she's going to be fine. I just need to get through this first.*

"I wish I could've met your friend." My grandmother's voice was wistful, snagging my attention. Her eyes twinkled with mischief, and I was reminded of all the times she'd cheered my sister and me on as we'd concocted one plot or another behind my mother's back.

I turned my attention back to the present. "What happened after you followed Aldea?" I looked around the room we were in. "How did you get here?"

She stared out the window for a second before answering. "Word got back to the Enclave about what I was doing here. I was making waves, you see. Stirring up trouble." Grandma Dottie smiled ruefully. "I'm afraid you come by that particular trait naturally."

I wasn't ready to bond over shared character traits yet, so I bit my lip. "Go on."

"How much do you know about the Enclave?"

"A little," I said. Craig had given me the quick-and-dirty rundown, so I knew the Enclave was the ruling body for all supernaturals. "Rumor has it that there is one representative for every faction—shifters, witches, vampires, and necromancers."

"That's correct. There are also three seers who serve in the Enclave."

"Okay." I wanted her to get back to the pertinent part of her story—the part where she decided that allowing me to believe she was dead was acceptable.

She reached for my hand but thought better of it when I stiffened. "When one member of the Enclave dies, another representative is chosen by the seers."

I frowned. That differed from what was commonly believed. "The factions themselves have no say in their representative?"

"No. Only the seers determine who will be called to serve."

"And you were called?"

She nodded. "I was."

Some of the tightness that had wound its way around my heart softened. *Maybe she hadn't had a choice.*

Grandma Dottie must have seen the relief on my face because she jumped in before it could grow. "I was given a choice, Kali."

The tears I'd been fighting tracked down my cheeks. "You chose this."

"I did." This time when she reached for my hand, she didn't allow me to pull away. "I'm sorry, but it was the only way I thought I could get justice for Claire." She searched my face, hoping for an understanding I was incapable of granting her just now. "It was the only way I thought I could protect you."

I jerked my hand back. "Protect me?"

"Yes," she said, but she had guilt written all over her face.

"How did you think locking yourself away on some remote island halfway around the world would protect me? Because let me tell you, it did nothing to protect me." The crow pulsed with my rising anger, a thrum on my chest that I didn't bother to tamp down. "Do you know who did protect me?" I challenged. "My friend Riley protected me by showing up with a flamethrower and a handful of fricking smoke bombs to face a demon. For me. Craig put himself in the line of fire. He took a bullet for me. Hell, even Volkov and Meira protected me in their own way. But you?" The tears came harder now. "You let me believe you were dead, knowing what your loss would do to me."

Grandma Dottie had helped put me back together after Claire died, and she'd been the one constant after my mother walked out on me. She'd known the devastation she would leave behind. And she chose it anyway.

Grandma Dottie tried to hug me—something she'd done hundreds of times over the years—but I jumped off the loveseat and backed away from her embrace.

"No." I ignored the flash of hurt that crossed her face. "You left me all alone." She opened her mouth to argue, but I cut her off. "There was no one left for me." I swept my arm around the room. "So, you could choose what? This?"

"Every choice comes at a price." Grandma Dottie stood up next to me, but she didn't reach for me this time. "I'm sorry you had to pay it, too."

"I'm too angry to speak to you right now. I need to be

alone." I stepped past her, stiffening at the familiar touch of her hand on my arm.

"Sweetheart, there are dangers out there that you are wholly unprepared for," she cautioned.

"And whose fault is that?" The words were out before I could stop them. We both knew I wasn't talking about the wildlife. She could have stayed all those years ago, told me what I was, trained me to prepare for what she knew would be coming for me. But here we were.

Grandma Dottie dropped her hand to her side and let me pass. "We'll talk when you've had some time to process."

I didn't answer. I needed to be anywhere but here at the moment, so I walked out into the unfamiliar terrain under the cover of night. And the further I got from the building, the more distance I wanted to put between us. I didn't bother looking for a path, just crashed through the trees. I ran until my lungs felt like they were on fire and my feet slid on the slick rock of the beach. Stopping at the edge, I sat and stared out at the moonlight reflecting off the dark sea. Not even Raum seemed to know what to say, so he kept quiet, feeding on the waves of grief and rage coursing through me.

I sat for hours until the cold numbed me, and still, I couldn't force my feet to go back. I'd spent years wishing for one more day with my grandmother, one more moment to share between us before I had to let her go. Now that I had it, all I could feel was the bitterness of being left behind. I let myself cry for everyone I'd lost.

Finally, the tears stopped coming.

I heard my grandmother's approach before I felt her beside me. "What happens when I leave?" I forced the question past my lips, even though I was afraid of her answer. "Will I see you again?"

"No." Her voice broke. "All we have are these three days together. When you leave, you won't remember me. They'll alter your memories so that I am not in them. When you think of your time at the Enclave, it will be as if you spent it with a stranger you can't quite recall."

"And you?" I asked. "Will you remember?"

"Always."

She sank to the ground next to me and wrapped me in her arms. I let her, and I cried again, this time for both of us.

CHAPTER 10

I woke in an unfamiliar bedroom, the soft sea breeze blowing the gauzy white curtains of the open window. It took me a few minutes to remember that I was in my grandmother's cottage on the island. I sat up and looked around. The morning sun was high enough in the sky to tell me I'd slept later than I had in months. Had I not been an emotional wreck, I might have even felt rested. As it was, my feet were heavy as I slid them to the floor and rubbed the sleep from my eyes.

Enough with the self-pity. I had access to an organization most of the supernatural world only mentioned in whispers. If anyone had answers about where to find weapons capable of killing Beleth, the Enclave would. And angry or not, I also had the gift of time with my grandmother.

Someone had dropped off clothing while I'd slept. I dressed quickly in the loose-fitting linen pants and pulled the light blue embroidered shirt over my no-nonsense white cotton bra. Someday, I was going to wear black lace pushup bras again that served no purpose other than to make me feel like a goddess. Despite the chipped pink nail polish on my toes, I grabbed the pair of gold sandals laid out next to my dusty boots and wished I had time for a pedicure.

I wandered out of the bedroom and found my grandmother reading in a comfortable chair like it was an ordinary day rather than the morning after she'd shattered my trust. She stood up when she saw me and moved toward the kitchen. "Are you hungry? I have muffins and fresh coffee."

I nodded curtly. I was still furious with her, but I wasn't foolish enough to pass up sugar and caffeine. Something told me I was going to need them to get through the day. Plus, it was hard to be angry with the smell of cinnamon and freshly brewed coffee calling my name.

She poured me a cup and set the coffee and a cinnamon streusel muffin on the small island that divided her galley kitchen from the rest of her cottage. Her cottage was small but cozy, with mismatched throw pillows and cheery paintings that I recognized as hers. Grandma Dottie had always painted for the joy of it rather than the end product. Most of her paintings looked like middle school art projects, but the vivid colors and bold designs brightened the space and made me think of my childhood.

I ignored the pang of nostalgia and got down to business. "Why did you bring me here?"

Grandma Dottie frowned and stared at my untouched muffin. "The Enclave wants to ensure that you are prepared to face Masterson." She looked up. "And Beleth."

"I see." I took a bite of the muffin, but it caught in my throat. I washed it down with hot coffee, not caring that it burnt my tongue. The sting gave me something to focus on, at least.

I squared my shoulders. "Let's get this evaluation over as quickly as possible, then. And when we are done, I want the Enclave to remove my restrictions and let me go home."

"I can't promise you that," Grandma Dottie said. "The Enclave must be sure you are ready."

"You speak of them in third person, but you're one of them," I accused. "Will the other Enclave members be part of my evaluation?"

"No," she said. "They will remain in their own cottages during the time you're on the island."

"They trust you to be impartial?" That surprised me.

Grandma Dottie raised her chin. "They trust me to prepare you." She looked away.

At the mention of trust, the leash on my anger snapped, and Raum rose up to meet it. The coffee cup in my hand shattered. "Shit!" The coffee scalding my hand was enough to center me, and I pushed him down again.

Grandma Dottie rushed me to the kitchen and turned on the cold water like I was ten again. I turned my face, so she wouldn't see the tears I blinked away as she rinsed the coffee from my hands.

I pulled back and grabbed a nearby towel to dry my hands. "As long as I'm here or at the Compound, Drew is at risk."

Grandma Dottie put the shattered remains of my coffee cup in the trash. "Shadows have been assigned to protect your brother. I can assure you, they are the best of the best."

"Masterson got to Naomi inside the Compound. Forgive me if I don't want to risk the safety of my family to the best of their best." I knew I sounded bitter, but just because she was willing to entrust his life to paid assassins didn't mean I was. "Masterson wants Drew so that he can locate me. If he dies, it will be because of me."

"Kali—"

I held up a hand. "As soon as Masterson knows where to find me, I become his target, not Drew, and not Dad."

"I'll talk to the rest of the Enclave, but I can't make any promises," she said.

I wouldn't believe them even if you did. "We don't have a lot of time, so we should get started."

She looked like she wanted to say something, but whatever it was, she thought better of it. "You're right." She slid on her shoes and opened the door. "Come. There's something I need you to see."

Grandma Dottie's cottage was the furthest away from the main building, allowing me glimpses of the grounds as we walked. Grandma Dottie clearly wasn't the only person who lived on the island.

"How many people live here on the island?" I asked, trying to put aside my bitterness. I was still angry with her, but the truth was—angry or not—I loved her.

"Other than the Enclave members themselves, there are about twenty guards and staff who reside here year-round," Grandma Dottie said.

"Isn't that a security risk?" I asked, thinking of all the hoops Sato had jumped through to get us here.

"Everyone on this island is either an Enclave member or a Shadow. Some of those here have retired from field work but serve the Enclave in another capacity."

Grandma Dottie gave me a quick tour of the grounds that were open to me. I had free rein in her cottage and to the pool and grounds. However, I was only allowed in the main building when escorted by my grandmother. Likewise, I would have supervised access to the Enclave library, a stand-alone building located a short walk from her cottage.

The library was our destination today. Unlike the main building, with its modern construction, the library looked as if it had been standing on this island for centuries, forgotten by time. Cracks had formed in the foundation, and the tall windows banking the side of the building were narrow and tipped with Gothic arches. The glass was murky, allowing only glimpses of the dark bookcases inside.

We walked around the building, and Grandma Dottie stopped in front of a heavy wooden door. She smiled at me. "You are going to love this place. It's everything a magical library should be." She placed both palms against one of the sunken panels, and a warm glow backlit the door from around the cracks. When she removed her palms, the door swung inward on its own, granting us admittance.

I sucked in a breath as I surveyed the library. Grandma Dottie hadn't been exaggerating. This place was wondrous. Everything here was blanketed in soft light, and the air was laden with crackling magic. Tall shelves with rolling ladders lined the space as far as my eye could see. Besides the Gothic windows on the far wall, the top of the wall adjacent to the door was entirely glass. Below the windows, vining plants climbed the wall, and skinny espaliered trees grew to the ceiling, matching those growing on the outside of the building. In here, branches twisted in front of the glass and filtered the sunlight through their leaves.

"This is amazing," I breathed.

"Isn't it, though?" Grandma Dottie squeezed my hand. "Come."

We made our way deeper into the library to where a small table sat among cushioned chairs.

Her eyes dropped to the tattoo peeking from beneath the V-neck of my shirt. "First, I need you to tell me everything—

how you got that demon mark, the power and influence you've felt from it, and the visions you've been having."

I sat across from her and brought her up to speed. I didn't leave out anything, sharing what I knew about Raum and detailing my struggles managing the demon. When I told her about the push-and-pull between us, I confessed that sometimes he spoke to me. When I finished, Grandma Dottie was staring at me intently.

"May I see the mark?" she asked.

I pulled my shirt to the side, exposing the full tattoo. She stared at the largest crow, its eyes seemingly sentient within the ink. Around it were six smaller crows, some of which were perched on branches while others spread their wings in flight. Grandma Dottie reached out a finger to trace it, but she didn't follow the lines of the branches or the bodies of the crows. Instead, her cool finger outlined the mark below it— Zepar's mark. While it was visually obscured by the ink, the scarred skin was still raised beneath the tattoo. When she lifted her finger, I felt the burn of it against my chest.

Neither of us spoke for several minutes, each lost in our thoughts. She recovered first. "How hard does he fight for control?"

I tugged my shirt back into place. "When I feel particularly strong emotions, he's more present—through thoughts and driving actions before I can consider them." I thought about the times when he'd felt the strongest. Although he frequently pushed to the surface, he hadn't tried to wrest total control from me. Not like Zepar had. I frowned, trying to make sense of his actions. "Why hasn't he tried to take control of my body?" Maybe I should have asked him that question, but I wasn't ready to trust his answers. I looked at my grandmother's familiar face and wondered if I could afford to trust hers.

"Raum is not a typical demon," she said.

I snorted. The lobbying for a pet Chihuahua gave that away.

Grandma Dottie looked at me questioningly, but I waved for her to go on. "As you've probably guessed, Raum is a particularly skilled divination demon. He's also a bit of an odd duck."

A duck? I felt Raum's outrage through our bond, even though I clamped down on the connection.

"How so?"

She smiled. "Apparently, he was a bit on the eccentric side, for a demon. Raum has an affinity for humans and has a reputation for willingly jumping into host bodies when it suites him despite being strong enough to resist should he want to. At one time, he had a fondness for fortune tellers and gladiators."

"Why does that not surprise me?" I muttered.

Grandma Dottie continued. "He's skilled at all types of divination, but his favorite seems to be scrying."

That explained the orb. But none of this information was in the demonology books we'd searched. "How do you know all of this?"

Grandma Dottie shifted uncomfortably, and I narrowed my eyes. She was hiding something.

"I understand that Raum has shown you memories of Beleth fighting with the weapons that kept him in power." She didn't wait for an answer. Instead, she stood and walked to a nearby bookcase, pulling a thin volume from the shelf as if it were an old favorite. "To understand the vision, you need to understand demon hierarchy."

I sat up straighter as she laid the book between us. She flipped it open to a bookmarked page. "This is what we've pieced together of demon lines. It's as close to a genealogical record as we can get."

I studied the open pages. It was less a family tree and more of a listing. I ran my finger down the handwritten names until I located Raum among them. "So, this is Raum's family?"

"Not family, exactly. Demons belong to legions. As far as we can tell, each legion is made up of a type of demon, so each section of this book is organized by legion." She pointed to the list Raum's name was on. "The demons in this particular legion are divination demons." She flipped through the pages, pausing to point out each type of demon. "We've identified six legions. In addition to diviners, there are demons that deal in temptation, vengeance, war, deception, and chaos. Each legion is led by a demon king." Grandma Dottie tapped a symbol drawn at the top of the page.

I studied the symbol. "That's Beleth's sigil."

"Yes. Beleth led the temptation demons. The artifacts Raum showed you—a war scythe, a dagger, and a shield—are how he consolidated power. The scythe and dagger were supposedly forged in hellfire millennia ago by the first demon king and tempered in his blood."

I scowled. *Ewww.*

Grandma Dottie patted my hand awkwardly before continuing. "They are rumored to be the only two weapons able to kill demons. The shield was forged from the same hell-fire and steeped in demon magic to protect against any weapon, including the scythe and dagger. Possessing all three made Beleth virtually indestructible. He proclaimed himself High Demon King and ruled the demon realm for centuries with an iron fist."

"He sounds like a real ass." Given my run-ins with him, it must have been a core personality trait.

Yes, Raum agreed, projecting an image of a donkey's ass.

Thanks for that visual, buddy.

But he wasn't done. The next image he sent was of Beleth sitting on the most atrocious throne I'd ever seen. All around him were the bodies of demons he'd hacked into pieces. The war scythe rested against his knee.

Grandma Dottie interrupted the show-and-tell. "Kali?"

I shook my head. "Sorry. Just thinking." I cleared my throat and studied the lists of demons. "Obviously, he lost the weapons somehow, or he wouldn't be here." I yanked on the connection, hoping to get a straight answer out of the demon. *What happened?*

Raum didn't disappoint. *The other kings rebelled. They used our strengths and planted spies close to Beleth. They waited years, until he let his guard down, then they stole the weapons.*

Grandma Dottie sighed. "There's no record of what happened to the weapons, but if what your demon said is true, they must be in the human world."

We hid them here, Raum admitted.

Why not just kill Beleth and be done with it? I asked him. They had the weapons capable of doing it.

He disappeared, Raum said. *After bitter fights for control, the remaining kings split up the demon artifacts and hid them.*

Wait. Artifacts? There are more than just the weapons and shield? I asked.

Oh yes, he said reverently. *There were many objects of power that the demon kings hid away to prevent another king from gaining that kind of power again.*

But they all wanted such power? I questioned.

They are demons, he said, and that was answer enough.

Right now, I needed to focus on stopping Beleth. I'd have plenty of time to worry about the other demon kings getting their hands on the artifacts once this fight was over.

CHAPTER 11

The door opened, and a young woman poked her head inside. "Are you ready for me?" she asked.

Grandma Dottie stood up and motioned her over. "We are." She turned back to me. "Kali, this is one of our resident witches. Before I can show you the Enclave's resources, you must swear a blood oath to guard the secrecy of their existence."

I watched the witch ready her supplies, which included a small scroll and a sharp dagger. "How can I battle whatever is coming if I can't share any of the information I find here?" I was only going to be here for three days. After that, I'd go back to the Compound and eventually to my life, and that's where I'd have to battle whatever was headed our way.

Grandma Dottie and the young witch exchanged a look.

"I didn't say you couldn't speak of the information," my grandmother said. "But you won't be able to discuss where the source of that information is located."

I frowned. "Sato said my memories would be altered to

ensure I couldn't find this island again. Why do I need to swear a blood oath as well?"

Grandma Dottie sighed. "It's an added precaution."

When I made no further objections, the witch unrolled the scroll and pointed to the bottom. "This is where you'll sign."

I read the document, and when I was satisfied that it was standard oath fare with no weasel words sprinkled in, I reached for the dagger and stared at it dubiously. *How exactly does one sign in blood, anyway? I have a hard enough time signing credit card readers with a stylus.*

"You don't need to actually sign your name," Grandma Dottie explained. "Just prick your finger and press it on the line."

I followed her instructions and handed the signed scroll back to the witch. She put it in her pocket for safekeeping and then reached for my hands. I hesitated, looking at my grandmother.

"She's going to do a binding spell if you'll let her. It will make it easier to keep your oath. Any time you attempt to talk about the items you see here anywhere except on these grounds, the spell will bind your tongue to prevent you from saying anything that could give away the location of these items."

"Okay." I extended my hands to the witch.

Instead of holding them, she pressed my palms together and wound them with a thin length of jute to symbolize the binding. Then, she placed her hands on the outside of mine and began the incantation. I felt a buzz where the jute touched my wrists. It traveled throughout my body before dissipating.

"All done," the witch said cheerfully. She looked to my grandmother. "And the other spell?"

Grandma Dottie's jaw tightened. "I spoke to the rest of the

Enclave about cutting your training at the Compound short. Unfortunately, that will not be possible. They've arranged for a blood cloaking spell to ensure Masterson cannot locate you."

The witch reached for me, and I bared my teeth, rage coursing through me. "A blood cloaking spell does nothing to protect Drew." I wasn't naïve enough to believe the cloaking spell was for my benefit either. They offered it as a means to protect the location of the Enclave and the Compound.

"It's the best I can offer," Grandma Dottie said quietly.

"It is not good enough." I turned on the witch, who shifted nervously from foot to foot. I let Raum thread my voice with his power. "Get out."

She gathered up her things and left as quickly as she could.

"Kali, I don't have a choice, here." Grandma Dottie reached for me but thought better of it when she saw my face.

I took several minutes to get myself under control again. "Let's go see whatever it is that you brought me here to see." The sooner we got this over with, the sooner I could jump through their next hoop and get out of here.

Grandma Dottie took a deep breath. "This way."

We made our way to the back of the library where a slightly smaller bookcase was recessed into the wall. My grandmother's eyes lit up as she reached for a book on the shelf above her head.

"Is that what I think it is?" When I was younger, I'd been obsessed with the idea of secret passageways and hidden libraries. Claire and I had spent days designing our perfect home using colored pencils and a giant sketchbook while our grandmother looked over our shoulders.

Instead of answering me, Grandma Dottie smiled and pulled the book. Sure enough, it tilted instead of coming off the shelf. The lever released the lock mechanism, and the entire bookshelf swung out, revealing the secret room hidden behind it. Old-fashioned torches lined the walls, and a large wrought-iron chandelier dotted with candles hung from the ceiling.

All of them lit as we entered the room. "How?"

She leaned closer to me. "Magic. The lever triggers it."

Of course.

This room was smaller than the outer library, but it was still a large room. There was a countertop-height wooden library table in the center of the room but no chairs to be found, which meant this room was not intended as a place to linger. Instead of bookcases, open shelving lined three of the walls. The other wall was empty save a nearly floor-to-ceiling oil painting of a tree.

"That's a weird place for a painting of a tree," I noted.

Grandma Dottie gave me a sharp look, and I felt like I was eight again, being admonished for telling a shopkeeper her porcelain doll collection was creepy. The dolls had been creepy, and this was a weird-ass place to hang a painting.

"Don't worry about the painting. Here's what you need to see." She was standing in front of the shelves, which held plain cardboard boxes of various sizes. Each box was labeled with a series of numbers and letters that meant nothing to me as I tried to decipher them.

"What's in these?" I asked.

My grandmother pulled out a black three-ring binder and placed it on the table. "This room is where we house magical artifacts that are deemed too dangerous for the general public."

I arched a brow. "The general public?"

"The general supernatural population," she clarified.

Grandma Dottie scanned the directory until she found

what she was searching for. Then, she mumbled the combination of letters and numbers under her breath as she went to hunt down the item.

"What kind of things?"

Her shoulders drooped as she lost the numbers she was reciting. "Damn it, Kali. Shhhh." She looked at the directory again and returned to the seemingly endless row of boxes until she found the one she had been looking for.

This time, I waited until she had it in her hands to repeat my question. She unfolded the flaps of the box and pulled out a velvet-lined case so old it belonged in a special museum collection somewhere with humidity control. Oblivious, she set the glass case on the table and unlatched the top, reaching inside and pulling out a small glass orb the size of a snow globe. The glass was clear with the exception of the living flames that danced inside it. She handed it to me.

The demon stirred inside me, and a charge like static electricity raced through my skin where it touched the orb. The crow beat its wings against my chest in agitation. *Thief!* Raum yelled. *That does not belong to her. It's mine.*

This was the scrying orb Raum needed to find the weapons capable of killing Beleth. Excitement thrummed through me. Finally, something we could use to go after him rather than waiting for him to make his next move.

I held up the orb. "How did you get this?"

"It was hidden in a cave in Peru, guarded by vampires. When it came to our attention, we secured it and brought it here."

Dirty thief. Raum's anger pulsed against the bond.

Simmer down, I told him. *We have it now.*

I stared transfixed at the flames flickering beneath the glass. "It's beautiful."

Grandma Dottie watched me handle it, turning it over in my palm so I could examine it from every angle. She plucked the orb from my hands and set it on the table.

"Scrying has been used for centuries for divining."

"How does it work?" I asked, staring into it again.

"People scry to envision the future, to seek understanding, or to see things more clearly." Grandma Dottie leaned down and looked at the flames with me. "Scrying usually involves looking into a reflective surface—often water or fire—to focus visions. Witches use the method frequently to seek clarity or direction. They put themselves into a meditative state by looking into whatever they're using to scry with, and as they stare into the surface, they see visions."

"And this will show me where to find the weapons?" I lobbed the question out there, not caring which of them answered.

Yes, Raum insisted.

"Maybe," Grandma Dottie said at the same time. "Often, scrying visions leave a lot to interpretation. What you see might just be a form in the flames or a blurred picture in the surface of rippling water. For the witches, at least, it's a bit like a Tarot reading. They use it more as a guide than a full picture."

I tapped the glass. "And this flame?" I suspected I already knew what it was. The pull it had on me was a hint.

"Hellfire," Grandma Dottie confirmed. "According to the demon texts, this orb belonged to Raum. Only a divination demon can use it. To anyone else, it's just a pretty oversized marble."

"And you think because I'm bonded to Raum, I'll be able to use it?" Raum had certainly implied that I could use it when he'd demanded I find it.

"There's only one way to find out." She shoved the orb into my hands and sat back to watch.

I hoped being bonded to a demon would allow me to use it as a proxy. When I felt calm enough, I raised the scrying orb in front of me and stared into the flames. Then, I pictured Beleth's weapons, but nothing happened. *How does this work?* I asked Raum.

Not here, Raum whispered. *We must not tell her where to find the weapons, or she will take them as she did this orb.*

I wanted to argue, but I didn't know if he was wrong. Even though I watched the flames for a long time, no visions came. No matter how many times I tried, the only thing I saw when I looked into the orb was my own reflection. Raum's silence was absolute. There was no way he'd help me use the orb as long as we were under the Enclave's watchful eyes.

I looked at Grandma Dottie. "I need to take this with me."

She shook her head. "I'm afraid that's not possible. The Enclave won't allow it to leave this island. You'll have to use it here."

We'll steal it back, Raum said.

As if she guessed my intention, Grandma Dottie sighed. "Sato will search you before you leave the island. There's no way you will get an object like this past him."

Then, we kill him, Raum said matter-of-factly.

I coughed. Even if I wanted to kill Sato—which I didn't—it would take a lot more than a midlist demon to take that man out. Our only chance of leaving this island with the orb was to get the Enclave to make an exception. Hopefully, they wanted me to find those weapons more than they wanted control. Given my previous experiences with the powers-that-be, I wasn't overly optimistic about the chances of that.

"Raum doesn't trust you." I ran a fingertip along the glass

and avoided looking at her, so she wouldn't read the echoing distrust in my eyes. "He won't help me as long as we're here."

"I see." Her voice caught. "We'll think of something." She put the orb back in its case and retrieved a book from one of the shelves.

I peered over her shoulder. "What is that?"

"This particular book is one from a set deemed too dangerous to leave these shores." She turned the book so I could see the spine, which had a four etched into it. "We haven't found all the books, but this one came to us from right here in Bucharest."

Raum rumbled under my skin. He didn't have to say it for me to know that this was another of the demon artifacts brought to our world to keep out of Beleth's hands.

"And it's dangerous?" I knew as well was anyone how dangerous some books could be in the wrong hands. Samara's grimoire was an example of that. But this book didn't look like a grimoire. For one, it was numbered. "Does it contain black magic spells?" *What would we need with black magic spells?*

"Not this one," she said, implying that others did. "This book contains demon history." She laid it back on the table and waited for me to pick it up. "It's dangerous because of who wrote it."

I fingered the cover, but as soon as I touched it, I jerked my hand back, repelled. Raum's bond, on the other hand, hummed at its nearness. "A demon wrote it?"

She nodded. "Yes. It is one of several demon artifacts smuggled out of the hell realm that we've brought here for safekeeping."

I grabbed the book and bent over the page, but whatever language it was written in wasn't one I recognized. "How are we supposed to read this?"

Instead of answering, she consulted the directory again, then pulled another box off a lower shelf. Inside the box was a brass monocle nestled in a velvet case. Grandma Dottie lifted it out and looked through the lens at the page. "Try this." She handed me the monocle.

I moved closer to the page. As long as I looked through it, whatever magic the monocle held translated the demon text into English. I whistled. "That's handy."

Since neither of us could read demon language, we traded off the monocle, with one of us reading and the other gleaning what she could from the abundant—and often grotesque—illustrations.

We spent most of the day skimming the demon history book. Most of it corroborated what Raum had already told me. Despite her sharing this book, I couldn't shake the feeling that my grandmother was hiding something. When I asked if the Enclave had anything else that could help us track down the weapons, she hesitated long enough I didn't believe her when she said there was nothing. Trust between us was tenuous as it was. We didn't need any more secrets between us.

That night, I tossed and turned as dreams of the first demon war haunted my sleep. Eventually, the dream shifted, and I was back in Kansas City at my shop. I heard a commotion outside and went to look. Outside, Beleth walked down the street in full demon form, trailing fire and brimstone in his wake. All manner of grotesque hybrids trailed after him as they lay waste to the city. Beleth's head swiveled toward me like an owl's, his eyes burning in his skull. As our eyes met, he smiled and raised his war scythe into the air as he passed by.

I woke before dawn drenched in sweat, with a burning in

my chest that warned me Raum was not content to remain dormant any longer.

Come, Raum whispered. *We need to look while we are not being watched.*

I wasn't in the mood to deal with Raum, so I tried to slam our bond shut as I sat on the edge of the bed and rubbed the tattoo. No matter how hard I tried to close the connection, I couldn't repress him. I felt the tattoo lift from my skin and trickle like smoke around my fingers. When it reformed as a crow, it flew out my open bedroom window before I could call it back to me.

The other times the crow had left my body, it had been to scout ahead for me, to show me something I wanted to see. Now, the crow flew on its own, giving me the gift of its sight without any control over what it sought. The early morning sun was beginning to lighten the sky, but the grounds were still cast in shadows.

Without hesitation, the crow flew directly to the library. When it reached the building, it disintegrated into smoke and reformed on the other side of the wall. The torches and candles flared for the bird just as they had for us, lighting the space.

The crow landed on a bookcase and turned its head as if to look at me. I felt Raum tug against the bond, like he was trying to get me to follow the crow's path. When I remained on the edge of my bed, the crow took flight again, this time seeping around the cracks in the bookcase that served as the door to the artifact room.

The crow bypassed the shelves of artifacts and landed on a decorative tile inlaid on the otherwise plain floor. Although the tile was the same color as the surrounding ones, it had a faint recessed design that I hadn't noticed before. *Why would someone put a single decorative tile there?* I wondered. It wasn't even in the center of the floor but rather next to the wall, directly below the oil painting of the tree. The crow gazed down at the decorative tile long enough to make sure I saw it, then he went through the painting.

A pair of magic-fueled torches cast the small room beyond the painting in flickering light. The room was sparse. The bird landed on a wooden podium that held an open book. Although the crow peered down at the pages, it was written in the same demon language as the history book Grandma Dottie and I had been studying. Whatever was in this book was important enough that the Enclave had hidden it behind two layers of secrecy on an island no one could get to without a personal escort from the most feared assassin in the supernatural world.

I needed to know why.

CHAPTER 12

$\mathcal{I}$ dressed quickly and tossed my sandals out the open window before climbing out myself and dropping barefoot to the ground. It was still early enough that I was alone on the grounds. To be safe, though, I stayed close to the building then edged along the tree line to reach the library, keeping to the shadows as best I could. When no one raised the alarm, I mimicked Grandma Dottie by pressing my palms to the door panel. Magic zapped my palms, and I jerked my hands back. *So much for the easy way.*

I circled the perimeter of the building looking for possible access points. There were no obvious contenders. What I wouldn't give for a simple back door and Riley's lock picking kit right about now. I bit my lip as I considered my options. A tug on the bond made me tilt my head up. The crow perched on the only way to get inside without an escort—the high windows propped open to let in the island breeze. Those windows, however, happened to be ten feet off the ground. If it weren't for the espaliered trees lining the wall, I wouldn't have considered it.

I stared at the crow above me. "Can't you open the door with your demon magic?"

Its only answer was to hop off the ledge and disappear back into the library. *Thanks a lot.*

I rubbed my palms on my pant legs and psyched myself up. *I can totally do this.* Kicking my sandals under a bush, I tested my weight on the forked limbs. When it held, I grabbed a higher branch and found another foothold. It took me a long time to reach the window because I was certain each new branch would buckle under my weight. Only one cracked, and I was able to shift my weight to another before I could crash to the ground. Finally, I grabbed a branch above my head with one hand and the window ledge with the other.

While the window was propped open, there would barely be enough space to squeeze through. I'd have to first hoist myself onto the sill before wiggling through to the other side. *On the bright side, three weeks of Aleksei's torture calisthenics are finally going to pay off.* Not one of those pushups or pullups would be in vain. Without them, no way in hell I'd be getting inside this library. *I've got this.*

It took a couple tries, but I hoisted myself onto the sill. Because the windows were long and narrow, I went through sideways, hooking my left leg over the ledge. Once through, I fumbled for a foothold on the other side. I lowered myself until my foot found a sturdy resting place and breathed a bit easier. I looked below me, the lit torches and candles inside helping me map my way down.

Impatient with my snail's pace progress, the crow flitted around my head before landing on a branch next to my face. It ruffled its feathers as if irritated I was taking so long.

"Some of us don't have wings," I muttered. Its beady eyes

were judgy as it swiveled its head in my direction. I flapped my hand at it. "Shoo, you little demon bird."

When he didn't budge, I swatted in his general direction until he took flight. Unfortunately, the movement threw off my balance, and my right foot slid off the small branch it rested on. I managed to grab the branch above me to stop my crash landing, but not before I slammed my chin against the bark.

The crow swooped above me in a blatant aerial celebration. *What an asshole.* Just to spite him, I slowed my descent.

After climbing the rest of the way down, I hustled into the artifact room, my crow hovering overhead. I faced the oil painting, noting that the decorative tile on the floor was close enough to the wall to assure no one stepped on it by accident. I stood on it until I heard the click of a latch being released. Tired of waiting for me, the crow slid in through the crack. I gripped the frame and pulled the painting toward me like a door before stepping into the small room.

The crow had once again landed on the podium and was waiting for me. As soon as I approached, the crow disintegrated and sank back into my skin, leaving me alone with the book it wanted me to read. I leaned toward the book, a chill pricking my skin as I examined the demon language.

Even though I knew I was stalling, I checked the cover. It was identical to the demon history book, its only distinguishing feature the number five on the spine. This was the book that came after the history of the first demon war, then. The war that Raum showed me in a memory.

They don't want you to see this, Raum insisted. *You are the destroyer, and you have a right to know what has been foretold.*

I opened the cover and flipped to the first page, anticipation building inside me. I had to know what it said, what they would keep from me. Frantically, I searched for the brass monocle we'd used earlier to read the demon text. I couldn't find it.

You have no need of the monocle, Raum said. *It is in my language. I can read the prophecy for you.*

My heart raced at the prospect of ceding more control to Raum, but the need to know what this book said overrode my fear. I loosened my hold on the bond, feeling him swell inside me. When he began reading the prophecy, he pitched his voice deep and soothing as if reciting a lullaby to a child.

Beware the dangers born unto the human world,
twins birthed on the eve of a new moon
with power unlike the world has seen
for they shall be able to call forth demons
and command whole armies of the dead.
When they come, it will be as
the innocent child and the sacrifice,
as the corrupter and the destroyer.
Only the strongest among them shall survive,
two souls bound through magic and bathed in blood,
and the fate of our world shall rest with the victor.

The beginning echoed Meira's continued insistence about my abilities being stronger than other necromancers and her prediction that I could call forth demons and command armies of the dead. *Had she known about the prophecy somehow?* The room grew stifling as I read the prophecy again, each word heavier than the last.

Destroyer, Raum said reverently, while every shitty thing that had happened in my life slid into focus. This wasn't the first time Raum had called me that, but this was the first time I understood what it meant.

When the sound of footsteps grounded me back in the present, I didn't turn around. This prophecy wasn't something I could unsee, and I wasn't about to pretend otherwise. Grandma Dottie stopped abruptly when she reached the open doorway. I hadn't bothered to close the painting behind me.

"Kali—"

"You kept this from me, too." Numbness settled in. I turned around. "Why?"

Grandma Dottie looked from the prophecy to me. She closed her eyes, and her voice shook. "Prophecies aren't set in stone, Kali. We can change it."

"Can we?"

"We can change it," she said more firmly. She reached for me, flinching when her hand touched mine.

I knew what she felt. My demon had flooded the bond until my eyes surely bled black, and I let him, borrowing his strength to bolster my own. "If you thought we could change it, why hide it from me?" My voice came out deeper, tinged with a demon's compulsion.

Grandma Dottie's eyes widened, but she answered immediately. "I didn't want you to carry that burden."

Seeing the pain twisting her features, I took a few deep breaths until Raum receded, and I was firmly in control again. "How many people know what I am?" I stared at the words that were once again in an unfamiliar language. "Other than the demons who recorded it, who knows?"

She glanced down at the book before meeting my eyes. "The Enclave has had this book since before you were born. When they received word Claire was killed, they had you watched."

"The innocent child and the sacrifice," I whispered, swallowing against the lump forming in my throat. "They had me watched?"

"Yes," she said. "Shadows were assigned to monitor you for signs that you were coming into your powers."

"And when I did?"

She stared at the floor. "The kill order was on the table when I was recruited. The minute you displayed your powers, they would have called it in."

I gasped. "That's why you joined them. You did it to shield me."

Grandma Dottie squared her shoulders. "I wasn't about to lose another granddaughter."

Some of the old hurt drained out of me. I slammed the link with Raum closed, not wanting him to taint this conversation.

"And that's all it took? You joined the Enclave, and they looked the other way?" I studied my grandmother, wondering what kind of power she possessed to make recruiting her valuable enough to risk me ending the world.

"Nothing so simple as that. When I accepted the Enclave's invitation, the kill order was placed on hold, and I was in a position to ensure it stayed that way." With one last look at the demon prophecy, she turned and walked out of the room. "Come, sit with me," she coaxed.

I followed her into the main library room, dropping into one of the chairs next to her. I ran my fingers through my hair as I tried to make sense of it all. "You wrote the letter you left for me before you came to Romania—before you knew any of this." I looked up for confirmation. At her nod, I continued. "If coming into my powers was the catalyst for the kill order, why not just stop Meira from training me in the first place?"

"I wasn't allowed to communicate directly with Meira."

I gripped the edge of the table. "Did Meira know you were alive?"

Grandma Dottie shook her head. "No. She thought I was dead, just like everyone else. The best I could do was send word through the Shadow assigned to monitor you that Meira should concentrate on teaching you to control and shield your magic, not strengthen it." She frowned, a flash of anger crossing her face. "She didn't listen."

While Meira had always paid lip service to my need to control my magic, she'd never mentioned anything about shielding. But that wasn't the part I got hung up on. "Wait. A Shadow was assigned to me after I moved to Kansas City?"

Grandma Dottie looked away. "Yes."

"Would this be the same Shadow that had been assigned to me in Chicago?"

"No," she admitted. "Someone new."

"Someone able to carry out the kill order," I finished for her.

She nodded slowly.

"Who?"

Grandma Dottie balled her hands into fists on her lap. "I can't share that information."

"Can't or won't?"

"Can't." She grimaced. "I'm bound by magic not to disclose the identities of any Shadows. Without those oaths, none of our Shadows would be safe from persecution. I'm sorry."

I stood and paced to the other side of the room, the sudden need for space overwhelming. I ran through the possibilities in my mind. The only Shadow I knew was Liv, but she hadn't been in Kansas City when I'd arrived. It couldn't have been her. Logically, I understood it could have been anyone—

the delivery guy, a neighboring business owner, the woman at the corner salon who cut my hair. But it could also be one of the two men who had been trained at the Compound.

Craig Ward and Max Volkov had admitted to training at the Compound as teenagers. Both men possessed the skills and the access to carry out such an order. Both had alluded to leaving it behind, but had they?

I could live with Volkov being the Shadow. We were barely civil to one another on a good day. But the thought of it being Craig felled me. I didn't want to believe he would have kept something like that from me or that the hands that held me had been poised from the beginning to end me. It didn't matter to my heart that by the time Craig and I had started dating, the order would have already been rescinded. It didn't make the possibility it was him any less devastating.

I turned back to face my grandmother. "The hit was called off?"

Grandma Dottie opened her mouth, probably to object to the word "hit," but reconsidered when she saw my expression. We were calling a spade a spade, here. "Yes. I convinced them to rescind the order."

"Why would they agree to that?" The Enclave didn't exactly have a reputation for leniency.

"I proposed an alternate strategy of containment."

"Let me guess. Surround me with Shadows."

She inclined her head.

"It doesn't make sense that they would agree to containment when they had the means of eliminating the threat. Why would they do that?"

Grandma Dottie stared at my shirt where it hid my tattoo. "A bigger threat took precedence."

I sat down again. "Let me guess. Masterson." Frederick

Parker Masterson was the man responsible for the demon tattooed on my skin. He'd been playing all of us for the last year, moving everyone like chess pieces until they were exactly where he wanted them.

"Beleth," she corrected, but they were essentially one and the same.

Beleth was the demon Masterson shared a body with. He'd summoned him decades ago in exchange for power and vengeance against a witches' council that had killed his lover Samara by sealing her in a cave and leaving her to die.

I'd been in this world long enough to figure out that the powers-that-be had more than enough capability to take on multiple threats at once. They didn't operate on any notions of mercy. If the Enclave rescinded the kill order on me, it was because they wanted something from me. "They knew Masterson wanted to use me, didn't they?"

She nodded.

"I was the bait."

Grandma Dottie leaned closer to me and pulled my hands into her lap. "Serving as bait bought us much-needed time." She squeezed my hands. "Time to figure out a way around that demon prophecy."

I held onto her hands, but I didn't share her optimism. The minute Claire died, my path had been set in motion. I now harbored a demon bound to my soul. Through magic and blood, I'd fallen lockstep in with the demon prophecy. *Corruptor and destroyer.* But as my grandmother searched my face with hope in her eyes and steel in her spine, I didn't have the heart to take it from her.

I forced a smile. "We have time," I agreed.

Despite the hollowness that took root inside me the minute I'd heard the prophecy, I did have time. I had the gift of another day with my beloved grandmother. I'd bask in every moment with her. When I left, and she faded back into memories, I'd find the war scythe and the dagger capable of killing a demon. I'd be the Enclave's weapon before he could make me his. I'd take Masterson out of this world, no matter what it cost me.

CHAPTER 13

"Are you sure you want to do this?" Grandma Dottie asked.

"I am." I was the only one who could take Beleth on, and we both knew it.

She disappeared into the artifact room and came back out a few minutes later loaded down with the demon texts the Enclave had in their collection, including the one with the prophecy. "If you're going after Beleth, you need to understand who he is, how he operates, and most importantly, what his weaknesses are."

"His weaknesses are the two weapons capable of killing him," I said.

Grandma Dottie stacked the books in front of me. "You're going to have to get close enough to use those weapons. To do that, you need to find the chink in his armor." She was right.

She pulled the brass monocle out of her pocket and handed it to me. Not wanting to rely on Raum's translations, I took it. After hours of searching, I closed the volume I'd been combing through and leaned back in my chair.

Grandma Dottie looked up from the book she was skimming.

I pointed to the three demon books the Enclave had recovered. Volumes one and six had yet to be found. While we had a dearth of information about demon history, missing the beginning and end volumes left a lot of gaps in our knowledge. At the moment, we were trying to locate as many references to the hidden demon artifacts as we could. There was a lot to sift through.

My top priority was locating the missing war scythe or the dagger. I'd already gone up against the demon once and failed to yank him out of Masterson. Even if I could strengthen my necromancy powers enough to successfully tear the demon out of Masterson and send him back to hell, I preferred not to take any chances that he'd find his way back. That meant I needed at least one of the weapons capable of killing him.

Securing the shield that could deflect such a weapon was also high on my to-do list. If I got my hands on the weapons capable of killing Beleth, I didn't want to chance him finding the shield and deflecting my blows. In addition to the weapons and the shield, there were also several mentions of other powerful artifacts that were taken from Beleth. Although the purpose each of them served wasn't always clear, they were mentioned enough that I didn't want to risk overlooking something that could prove important.

According to the text, the five remaining kings split the artifacts among them and then proceeded to squirrel them away in the human world for safekeeping. Unfortunately, there wasn't a demon artifact treasure map anywhere in these old books. Even the references to the artifacts were vague.

"There's too much information to sort through, and the mentions I have found are too vague to be helpful," I complained. "Even if the memory tampering doesn't muddle all of this in my brain, I'll never be able to recall most of it." I tapped my fingers on the thickest volume. "This would be a lot easier if you'd let me take these with me." Not only would it be handy to have reference books, taking them with me would mean more time now to talk about something other than ground demon horn and bloodletting before I had to say goodbye to my grandmother again.

Grandma Dottie passed me another book. "They'll never allow you to leave with these books."

"What they don't know…"

Grandma Dottie raised an eyebrow. "Even if you managed to smuggle the books out of this library, you'd never get them past Sato. The only way anything leaves the island is if the Enclave allows it."

I dropped my head onto the open book in front of me, groaning. "It was worth a shot."

Grandma Dottie patted my shoulder, and I sat up straight again as she dug in her pocket and pulled out a folded sheet of paper. My grandmother was a compulsive list maker, so she always had a few random sheets of paper stashed in her pockets. She tore off a quarter of the page and handed it to me.

"Umm, thanks?"

"Do you remember the time I had to pick you up from the principal's office?" We'd been reminiscing all morning as we searched the texts, but the question still felt out of left field.

"I do." I wondered where she was going with this. "You know, I was surprised you never told Mom and Dad about that."

She pointed her finger at me. "Snitches get stitches."

I laughed, as she probably had intended. The first time Grandma Dottie uttered that phrase was when Claire and I were kids. We'd spent the night at her house, and she'd let us stay up to watch horror movies until almost dawn. When she found out we had confessed to Mom, she'd leaned down and whispered it in a mock villain voice. After that, the three of us used it whenever someone let slip something they shouldn't have.

"Do you remember why you got in trouble?" she asked.

I snorted. "Seventh grade history."

She looked at the ripped piece of paper in my hand. "More specifically?"

"I got busted when a crib sheet I'd made for the test fell out of my pocket." The old middle school outrage welled up for a second. "I didn't even use it. I chickened out," I admitted.

Grandma Dottie handed me a pen. "You just needed an insurance policy to give you confidence."

I took the pen from her and stared at the thick books and the small slip of paper.

"Sato will search you," she warned, "so hide it well. Oh, and Kali?" She winked at me. "Write small." Although she'd never left me alone in here before, Grandma Dottie headed for the library door. "I'm going to go rustle us up some lunch."

Deciding what information was worthy of inclusion took longer than writing my notes. To pack in as much on one side as I could, I chose acronyms and symbols whenever possible. Each time I found a mention of a demon artifact in the texts, I drew a symbol to represent it.

Before Grandma Dottie came back, I also copied the prophecy word for word onto the back of the page. By the time Grandma Dottie returned, armed with a picnic lunch and bottled water, I'd already hidden my crib sheet. Turned out, a plain-Jane cotton bra could sometimes save the day. A little deconstruction of the lining, and I had the perfect hidden compartment for my demon notes.

My remaining time on the island passed quickly. Grandma Dottie and I took our picnic down by the sea and spent the time reminiscing about shared memories. She told me more about her childhood, including the discovery of her own necromancer powers and the years of training with her grandmother. Although my grandmother and I had always been close when I was younger, these conversations were different. They were as much about learning about each other as women as they were about dispensing whatever wisdom she could give me in our limited time together. Even though I knew they'd be stolen from me along with the memory of her when I left this place, I still cherished every detail I learned about her.

"How long have you known Meira?" I asked, curious about the woman Grandma Dottie had entrusted with my training.

"I've known Meira since we were teenagers." She looked out at sea as if she were recalling her younger days. "She was a lot different then—wild and reckless. She grew out of most of it."

I choked on the grape I'd been eating, and Grandma Dottie slapped me on the back. "Meira was wild?" The Meira I knew was the picture of stuffy decorum. The wildest I could imagine her getting was wearing white past Labor Day.

Grandma Dottie laughed. "I know what you're thinking, but it's true." She sobered. "She dabbled in some dangerous magic when we were younger, and I think it scared her enough that she was leery of anything that hinted at black magic after that."

I could see how a brush with darkness could turn Meira into the overly cautious woman I'd come to know. "Is that why you told me she was the only one I could trust in the letter you left me?"

Grandma Dottie shook her head. "That's not exactly what I said, Kali Rae." Unlike Claire, who had followed instructions to the letter, Grandma Dottie had often chastised me for playing fast and loose with her instructions when I was younger. Whether it was helping with Thanksgiving dinner or running to the corner store for her, she had insisted I repeat her instructions verbatim before she set me loose. She nudged my shoulder. "What did I say?"

I held my hands up in surrender. "You told me I could trust Meira to give me the tools I needed to use my powers."

"That's my girl." She ruffled my hair like I was a kid again. "Meira was the only necromancer I knew who would be strong enough to train you."

I thought back to the photo of the two of them at Claire's soccer game, heads bent together as they watched my sister play. The bond between them had been obvious, even from a photograph. "Is that why you had her evaluate Claire? Because Meira was powerful in her own right?"

Grandma Dottie frowned. "What do you mean?"

I told her about the photo I'd found of the two of them watching Claire's soccer game.

"Oh that," she laughed. "I forgot all about that visit. Meira showed up with a bottle of brandy and a tall tale about—" She glanced at me and laughed. "Well, let's just say she had unconventional tastes when it came to the men she dated."

I shuddered. "I don't even want to know."

"You really don't." She shook her head as if shrugging off the memory. "Now tell me about this man of yours. Does this gargoyle check all your boxes?" she teased.

When my sister and I were thirteen, we read some article

in a teen magazine that claimed the best way to find your perfect boyfriend was to list all the qualities you wanted him to have. Claire's list had been short and sweet—funny and kind, no chest hair, must like sports and dogs. Mine had been significantly more detailed, right down to the exact shade and style of blond surfer dude hair that he must have. Back then, I thought I wanted someone who would be the life of the party, who fit in with the boy bands I postered my walls with— someone who wouldn't take life too seriously.

"Not a single one." I bit my bottom lip. "Craig's completely bald." We both laughed until I had to wipe my eyes. "I could count the times I've seen the man laugh on two hands. But when he does laugh, it lights something up in here." I tapped my chest, all traces of laughter gone. "He's smart and strong. He's fiercely protective—sometimes annoyingly so—and loyal to a fault."

"And you love him?"

"Yes." I looked down at my lap. "But I'm afraid. He thinks I'm his mate. You probably know this, but gargoyles form soul bonds when they take a mate." I rubbed my crow tattoo. "How can I tie the man I love to a demon?"

"Oh sweetheart." Grandma Dottie pulled me in for a hug, and I rested my head on her shoulder. "One thing I know about gargoyles is that there's none of this wishy-washy thinking you're his mate. That man knows who you are to him, and there isn't a demon in this world he won't fight with you."

I swallowed past the lump in my throat. "I know." That was the problem. "What if I'm not strong enough to stay in control?"

Grandma Dottie squeezed my shoulder. "Then, you get strong enough because you're not just fighting for yourself anymore." We sat together, each of us lost in our own thoughts as we watched the waves lap against the shore. She stood, offering me a hand to help me stand. "We should go."

When I turned to look at her, the late afternoon sun bathed her face in a rosy glow that made my heart ache. She smiled back, but it didn't chase the sadness from her eyes. Saying goodbye today might be hard for me, but tomorrow, the loss would be an old hurt for me. For her, the wound would be new again.

An hour later, Sato knocked on her door. "It's time," he said.

Although I left in the clothes I arrived in, my grandmother insisted on wrapping me in an oversized sweater to ward off the chill from the sea. As expected, Sato searched me for smuggled goods. However, the crib sheet went undetected where it was tucked safely in my bra.

Grandma Dottie and I walked hand in hand all the way to the coast. When we reached the yacht, Sato gave us a minute to say our goodbyes.

I wrapped my arms around her, kissing her forehead the way she used to do for me when I was a kid. "I love you."

"Oh sweetheart, I love you, too." She brushed a hand across her cheek to wipe away an errant tear before pressing something into my hands. She pulled back enough, so I could see the orb she'd given me. I met her eyes and mouthed a thank you before tucking the orb into the folds of my bulky sweater. Grandma Dottie's eyes hardened, and she stepped back. "I am always in your corner."

I let her go.

Sato leaned over the railing and gestured for me to hurry up. Grandma Dottie cupped her hands to project her voice. "You make sure she's ready to face him." Her voice rang with authority, and Sato bowed in acknowledgement before busying himself preparing the yacht to sail.

The same witch who witnessed my blood oath waited for me on deck. After climbing aboard, I turned for one last look at my grandmother. Despite knowing I couldn't carry the image beyond these shores, I memorized the way she looked standing there, her arms braced at her sides while the wind whipped her hair around her.

Although the witch was just doing what she'd been ordered to do, I couldn't help but hate her as she touched my forehead to erase my grandmother from my memories of this place.

CHAPTER 14

This time, Sato's entrance into the Compound was a lot less splashy. Instead of dropping dramatically into the courtyard, we settled for walking through the front door. Even without the theatrics, everyone in the training yard stopped what they were doing to stare at us.

Before I could take more than a few steps inside, three furballs surrounded me. "Hey guys, you're looking good." I reached down and scratched the German Shepherd behind the ears. "Did you get baths?" The dogs were still skinny, but their fur was fluffy rather than matted, and some of the hollowness had left their eyes.

I glanced up to see Aleksei had joined us, looking fit for an international Fortune 500 reunion. "You have Quinton to thank for that." Sure enough, Quinton was lurking nearby, sporting a brand-new leather jacket that looked remarkably like the one I'd ruined.

"Thanks, Quinton."

Aleksei glared down at the dogs when they bumped into his perfectly pressed pant leg. He pointed at a mixed breed brown and white dog with soulful eyes and an overactive tail. "This one has a hurt paw. He can't stay here. He needs someone to nurse him back to health."

I didn't know what kind of shelters they had in Romania, but given the number of stray dogs in the tunnel, I didn't want to risk sending him to one. "I think Claudia would take him."

"The shopkeeper?" Aleksei asked.

"Yes. She lost her only daughter last year, and I know she's lonely. I think she'd give him a good home."

Quinton nodded solemnly. "I'll take him to her."

That settled, Aleksei gave Sato the side eye and a stilted greeting that had me wondering about their history. Sato kept his gaze straight ahead as he headed directly for Aleksei's office.

I caught Aleksei before he could follow him. "Any word on Riley?"

"No. I'm sorry." Aleksei turned toward his office. "Follow me."

Instead of following him, I pivoted toward my room, since the orb was still nestled under my sweater. I barely managed to keep my arms crossed over my chest to hold the orb in place. "Be there in a minute."

"In my office, now, Kali," Aleksei demanded.

"Gotta pee," I yelled over my shoulder as I hightailed it to my room before he could stop me. After hiding the orb in my underwear drawer, I headed back to join Aleksei and Sato. When I got there, Aleksei was sitting behind his desk while Sato stood with his back to the wall. The only thing that broke their frigid silence was the little dog who came barreling toward me from under Aleksei's desk.

I caught him up in my arms and stood, arching an eyebrow

at Aleksei. "Who's a good boy?" I cooed, rubbing behind the dog's ears while smirking at Aleksei.

"Are you finished?" he asked dryly. At my shrug, he gestured toward the chair. "Sit and tell me what you've learned."

I gave Aleksei the quick-and-dirty version of what I learned about Beleth and the first demon war, including the existence of demon artifacts that could be used to defeat him. I'd been battling a headache since we set sail, but it intensified as I recounted my visit with the Enclave. Aleksei studied me for a long time after I stopped talking, his pale blue eyes unnerving. I fought the urge to squirm under his scrutiny.

"And the Enclave is sending you to retrieve those weapons?" he asked.

I frowned. I may have rushed through some of the finer details, but that part of my story had been pretty clear. "Yes."

Aleksei turned his attention to Sato. "Are you accompanying her on this quest?" He couldn't quite hide the note of censure.

Sato answered without looking at either of us. "You know that I cannot."

"She's not ready," Aleksei protested, ignoring me altogether.

When Sato finally looked at Aleksei, the tension crackled between them. "Then, I suggest we get her ready."

Aleksei jerked back as if struck. "You're staying."

Sato stiffened. "I am. Is that going to be a problem?"

"Of course not," Aleksei snapped.

I had no idea what the charged subtext was beneath what they were saying, but I was certain this was more about whatever history was between them than my training. At the moment, though, my head hurt like someone had taken a hammer to it, so I didn't have the energy to sort it out.

"Alrighty then. I'll just leave you two to work out—" I waved my hand in their direction. "Whatever this is."

I ignored the sharp looks both men sent my way and didn't bother closing the door on my way out. When I made it to my room, I paused long enough to take a couple extra-strength painkillers before stumbling to my bed to sleep off the world's worst headache.

I didn't venture out of my room until the next morning. Both men were waiting for me in the courtyard. I may have thought training with Aleksei sucked, but I was certain that training with Aleksei and Sato would be a hundred times worse. We began with an evaluation.

"Why do we need to do this again?" I asked. "I should be focused on finding the weapons, something that I could do much easier if I wasn't wasting time with the two of you."

Sato and Aleksei exchanged exasperated looks. They may not have agreed on a lot, but they seemed pretty unified in their annoyance with me.

"Having the weapons won't do you much good if you are too weak to wield them," Aleksei said.

He wasn't wrong, so I gave their evaluation my best. Although Sato claimed the evaluation was to determine my strengths and weaknesses, there didn't seem to be many of the former. While Sato coolly demanded a demonstration of my combat skills, Aleksei circled me like a fully caffeinated drill sergeant, barking commands for me to move faster and hit harder. When the two of them weren't focused on me, they traded barbs and not-so-subtle putdowns like middle school mean girls. After an hour trapped in a room with the two of them, I'd had enough of their one-upmanship.

I staggered back to my feet after being thrown to the mat yet again. The two of them weren't even breathing hard, while I was gasping for air like a fish out of water. Their latest bickering match was over how we should spend the next hour. Aleksei argued we needed to cut straight to weapons training. Sato insisted we spend the time correcting the hand-to-hand techniques I'd picked up from inadequate training. From the looks of it, they were seconds from killing each other.

"This evaluation is over. I'm getting lunch."

I didn't wait for either of them to object, leaving with as much dignity as my bruised ribs allowed. When I got back to the training yard, Aleksei was nowhere in sight.

"We decided it would be more efficient to train you individually." Sato handed me a replica of the war scythe I'd seen in the demon texts.

I twirled it around like a baton, ignoring Sato's grimace. "Sweet." Unlike a traditional scythe, the blade was attached parallel to the long handle. The blade had a slight curve to it, like a crescent moon that tapered to a point. Even with a dulled training blade, it was an impressive weapon. The pole itself was thicker than the bo staff I was used to training with and over seven feet long.

Sato watched as I tested the weight of it, experimenting with different grips. "We're going to run through basics today."

"Basics?" I turned the weapon blade down and swung it like I was cutting grass.

Sato's hand snaked out faster than I could track, and he turned the weapon upright again. "You need to know how to hold the scythe properly and how to move with a large weapon without injuring yourself." He made me sound like a toddler with a steak knife.

"Okay, fine. And then you'll teach me how to fight with it, right?"

"Once you have mastered the basics," he agreed.

After an hour of walking around the courtyard carrying the weapon, Sato finally deemed me competent enough to learn basic movements. Whereas Aleksei's approach to weapons training usually consisted of tossing me the weapon of the day right before attacking me, Sato had me practice repetitive movements with the scythe.

My martial arts training before coming to the Compound consisted of classes at Craig's gym. Because Krav Maga was a mixed martial art focusing on self-defense and street fighting, I had zero experience performing katas. I rushed through my first attempts until Sato forced me to slow down and focus on precision with my movements. I spent the better part of the day twirling, stabbing, and spinning in slow motion.

When I got overconfident, Sato jumped in. "You're not in a marching band. Stop twirling it around like a baton." Periodically, Sato stepped in to adjust the angle of the weapon or to correct my hand position. "You're getting sloppy," he admonished, sliding my hands up a couple inches. "Pay attention to your grip."

I glared at him but dutifully adjusted my grip.

After a few more repetitions, Sato called time. "Tomorrow, we'll work on strike points and defense." He took the scythe from my hands and demonstrated again where he wanted me to hold it for various movements. "Tonight, I want you to mark your hand positions on the pole, so that you have a guide."

"Shouldn't we practice with a dagger, too?" There were two weapons capable of killing Beleth. It seemed logical to me to practice equally with both of them.

Sato gave me a once-over. "If you have to get close enough to Beleth to use a dagger, you're as good as dead." He handed me my war scythe. "Better to practice with the weapon you at least have a slim chance with."

"Gee, thanks," I called after his retreating back.

Liv caught me as I left the training yard where she'd been sparring for the last couple hours. "You gonna tell me why Mr. Intense is training you?"

Last night, I'd been too focused on eradicating my headache to chat with Liv, and today had been an all-day training marathon. My stomach rumbled, and I checked the clock. I'd missed dinner. "How about I catch you up over left-over pizza?"

"Deal."

I made a pit stop in my room to mark the correct hand positions on the scythe with tape before I forgot where they went. Then, Liv and I raided the industrial-sized refrigerator together, polishing off half a pepperoni pizza and several bottles of beer while we talked. Liv was perched on the steel countertop watching me demo my new weapon skills when Aleksei came looking for me.

He caught the scythe on a downward swing and yanked it out of my hands.

"Hey!" I protested, reaching for it.

Aleksei glared at the baby chick washi tape I'd used to mark the hand positions. "What the hell is that?"

I shrugged. "It was Sato's idea."

Aleksei handed the weapon back to me with a grimace. "Are you drunk?"

"No," I scoffed at the same time Liv shouted, "You betcha."

He pointed at Liv. "You, go sleep it off." He snapped his

fingers at me like I was a golden retriever. "And you, follow me. You've got a phone call to make."

I trailed after him. "Who am I calling?"

He didn't turn around. "Ward."

By the time we reached the communications room, I'd sobered enough to know a midnight call to Craig wasn't a good thing. "What happened?"

Since Aleksei and I were alone in the room without his computer guy to assist, Aleksei bypassed the fancy video-calling and pulled a nondescript cell phone out of the filing cabinet, turned it on, and handed it to me. "Just call him before he shows up on my doorstep."

I dialed his number, and he picked up immediately. "Craig?"

"Kali, are you okay?"

I laid the weapon on the computer table and sat down. "I'm fine."

"I called several times this week. Aleksei wouldn't put me through." Craig's frustration came through loud and clear.

"I'm sorry I worried you," I said.

I had tried to get Aleksei to let me call Craig before I left for the Enclave, but he'd said he'd take care of it. Since getting back, I had been preoccupied with training. And if I was honest with myself, I had been putting off the call because of the conversation I didn't want to have with him. Asking the man I'd finally let my guard down enough to love whether he was the one assigned a kill order for me wasn't something I was looking forward to. With Aleksei hovering nearby, now was not the time for that conversation, anyway.

"You sure you're okay?" Craig pressed when I was quiet too long.

No. I'm really not. "As good as I can be under the circumstances." I kept it vague, and he let it go.

I filled him in on where I had been and what I learned. The prophecy I kept to myself for now. That was a conversation I'd rather have in person. He was quiet for a long time, but I didn't know if it was from shock that I'd been summoned to the Enclave's location—a place that I couldn't recall getting to no matter how hard I tried—or from fear that I was planning on taking down a demon who had once reigned over hell. Either way, I didn't like the quiet.

"Are you still there?" I asked.

"I'm here."

"There's a lot still up in the air," I offered, knowing he needed time to process everything I'd just dropped on him. I changed the subject. "How's Riley? Did you find out where she was?" She was due back days ago, and I knew he would've checked on her.

Craig cleared his throat. "She's not back yet. She left Helen a voicemail saying there had been a complication, and she needed to stay off the radar for a while."

"When?"

"A couple days ago," he said.

"Craig, I'm worried she got in over her head. What if she's in real trouble?" I kicked the edge of the nearest computer table, frustrated I was stuck here while she was out there somewhere.

"If there is one thing Riley excels at, it's getting out of trouble. I'll let you know as soon as I know more," Craig promised. "Is Aleksei still there?"

I glanced at Aleksei, who was standing nearby, no doubt listening in on our conversation. "He's here. Hold on. I'll put you on speaker."

Craig switched out of concerned boyfriend mode and into enforcer mode the second he was on speaker. "I got a positive ID on that shifter from Kali's vision."

"Go on," he told Craig.

"He was a cougar shifter from Colorado. Went missing a couple weeks ago. His pack was small and pretty new, but…" Craig's pause told me the worst was yet to come. "He was the alpha."

"Fuck," Aleksei swore, looking at me. "Masterson is escalating."

"Looks that way," Craig agreed.

Aleksei's eyes were no longer pale blue. "Then, we don't have much time to get ready."

We said our goodbyes, and I stared at Aleksei. "I need to go home."

He looked at the practice scythe I held. "Whatever it was that you smuggled back from the Enclave, I suggest you use it to find the real one."

I scowled at him, imagining him rifling through my underwear to find contraband.

He tucked the phone back in the drawer. "You need to be more careful about those hall cameras," he tssked.

"Does Sato know I have it?"

"If Sato knew, you wouldn't still have it. Don't make me regret not telling him." Aleksei shut off the light, and I headed down the hall, my mind spinning.

Instead of going back to my room, I went to the training quad where Aleksei had brought me to practice control over Raum. At this time of night, the only people in the room were in containment cells or sick beds. I ignored all of them and headed to the meditation space.

I closed the drapes behind me and turned on the ocean

track Aleksei had used. After sitting down on the mat, I pulled the scrying orb out of my pocket and sat cross-legged on the floor. I tried to concentrate, but for some reason, the sound of waves crashing against the shore triggered a deep sense of sorrow. I stood and switched the ocean soundtrack for a crackling fire and tried again. This time, it only took a few minutes for me to settle. I reached for the bond, opening it wide enough that Raum's power flowed into me.

What do I do? I asked him.

Ask it to show you what you seek.

I didn't hesitate. *Show me Riley.*

Raum huffed but didn't object. I stared into the orb and pictured her face. It took several tries, but eventually, I saw her image in the flickering flames within the glass orb. She clutched some kind of blade in her hand while looking over her shoulder. Her eyes widened for a fraction of a second and then her image blurred and disappeared. I tried to recall the image for what seemed like an eternity, but nothing happened.

The sound of the door to the training room opening was my only warning that I was no longer alone. Hastily, I shoved the orb under a nearby throw pillow. I rested my hands on my knees, forming an o with my middle fingers and thumbs. My eyes closed just as the drapes parted.

"What are you doing?" Sato asked.

I cracked an eye open. "What does it look like? Meditation."

"You're meditating—in here—at midnight?"

"Looks that way," I said. "Aleksei has me do it when I can't sleep."

"Aleksei Volkov taught you to meditate?" Sato asked incredulously.

"Yup." I shut my eyes again and ignored him until he left. When I was sure he was gone, I tucked the orb under my shirt and hurried back to my bedroom to attempt sleep. Tomorrow, I was going to find a way to go home.

The next morning, I woke with a hangover and a growing sense of urgency. After a quick breakfast and a lot of water, I was back on the mat with Aleksei, who was demonstrating strike zones. When I rubbed my temples with a groan, he stopped jabbing the training dummy long enough to snap at me.

"You're not paying attention."

"I am," I argued, even though that was a stretch. Mostly, I'd been preoccupied with my lingering hangover and my worry for Riley.

Aleksei handed me the scythe. "Great. Then, you can demonstrate."

I used the end of the pole to demonstrate the strike zones as I called them out. "With the blunt end, I'd aim for the usual vulnerable spots—eyes, ears, nose, throat." I twisted the scythe and jammed it down, stopping an inch above his foot. "And, of course, a hard slam to the foot is always a good choice."

I'd paid less attention to Aleksei's instructions on using the blade, but since I wasn't about to admit it, I improvised. After adjusting my grip and stepping back, I swung the blade end toward the dummy. "With the blade, decapitation is the holy grail, but a strike to the back of the knees or slash to the hands can slow down even a demon." I adjusted my grip again, this time aiming at center mass as I stabbed the dummy with the tip-end of the weapon like it was a spear.

When it made contact, Aleksei snorted. "You're what, three feet from the target? How is it even possible to miss the heart?"

I started to object but then noticed that I was indeed stabbing the wrong side of the chest. "Oops."

"Practice." Aleksei left me alone as he wandered over to a group of soldiers who were sparring in the corner.

By the time Aleksei told me to knock off for the lunch, my arms were like dead weight at my sides. I buried my scythe in the target with the recognition that I was nowhere near ready to face Beleth. Not that it mattered. Practice was a luxury I could no longer afford.

CHAPTER 15

"**I** need to go home," I insisted.

I'd been arguing with Sato for the better part of the afternoon. Regardless of whether I was ready to face Masterson, I didn't want to hole up in a gym while he built his super army, my best friend was in who-knows-what kind of trouble, and my brother's life was in danger because Masterson didn't know where I was.

Because of the demon I was bonded to and the subsequent visions Raum brought with him, I was now useful to the Enclave. They needed me to hunt down Beleth's weapons and dispatch the demon while he was still only a thorn in their side rather than a bigger threat to the stability of the super-natural world. As long as they needed me, I had leverage—at least that was what I was telling myself.

I swung my war scythe, running through the set of moves Sato had taught me. "Thank you for training me as much as you have, but it's going to have to be good enough." I sped up my movements in an effort to show both men how much I'd learned.

"All a few days of training is going to do is get you killed," Sato warned. To prove his point, he attacked without his usual warning.

In a matchup between a war scythe and the humble bo staff, one would assume I'd have the advantage. But when Sato was the one wielding the bo staff, I didn't stand a chance. Unlike his slow-motion demos, he was a blur when he sparred. He came at me so fast, I forgot everything he'd taught me and reacted on pure instinct, bringing the scythe straight down toward his head like a battle ax.

Turned out, my instincts sucked. He caught the scythe easily with his bo staff. One quick twist, and I was weaponless. Before I could react, Sato spun behind me and took my knees out, then swung at my head, stopping the staff before impact to rest it against the back of my bent neck.

Aleksei crossed the room and stopped in front of me. "The problem is, you're still fighting like a human. You're never going to win a demon fight like that." He circled behind me, taking the bo staff from Sato's hands. Sato stepped to the side.

"Get up," Aleksei barked.

I jumped to my feet and grabbed my weapon. Aleksei didn't waste any time, attacking me with a ferocity that put me on my heels. Again and again, he struck. I deflected most of his blows, but barely. My arms ached from the effort of blocking his attack, and frustration made me sloppy. He took advantage, hitting me in the stomach hard enough to double me over.

Aleksei leaned down, so we were eye to eye. "Again."

I drew power from the demon, using the strength to move faster and strike harder. We traded blow for blow, my confidence growing as I held my own in the fight. I swung my scythe, landing a glancing hit to Aleksei's shoulder with the dulled blade.

"Better," he praised, right before he brought me to the ground with a combination of strikes I was wholly unprepared for. "But not good enough."

Sato was still watching us from the sidelines. "She's not ready."

"No," Aleksei agreed. "She's not."

"I'm getting better," I said stubbornly. I knew it was true, even if better wasn't good enough.

Aleksei didn't answer me. Instead, he reached down and plucked my weapon from my hands. Then, he gestured to Sato, who grabbed the spare war scythe from the courtyard's wall of weapons and joined us on the mat. I moved out of the way, taking up the spot where Sato had been observing us.

Sato moved with the scythe like it was an extension of him. As he tested the weight of it in his hands, his movements were a masterclass in combat.

Like everyone else in the training yard, I couldn't look away from the two men fighting. They were well matched. While Aleksei may not have been as fast as Sato, what he lacked in speed, he made up for in power. Today, both men were dressed in form-fitting black gym clothes. Watching them fight was like watching a choreographed dance that was equal parts beauty and brutality. I grabbed my water bottle and joined the crowd that had gathered on the other side of the courtyard to watch them fight.

After twenty minutes of trading blows, Aleksei and Sato called it a draw and hung up their weapons. They'd made their point. I had the fighting skills of a toddler compared to either of them.

I crossed the room to finish our conversation. They

exchanged a look when they saw me coming. If they thought a little display of their fighting prowess would cut our argument short, they didn't know me very well.

"Impressive," I admitted. "I'm sure it took you years of dedicated training to get that way. Unfortunately, I don't have years." I took my training scythe back from Aleksei. "You're both welcome to come to Kansas City with me to continue training, or you can call it complete. At the moment, I don't actually give a shit. Either way, I'm going home."

Sato's jaw tightened. "I can't leave the Enclave's location unprotected, and Aleksei is needed here."

"That settles it," I said cheerfully. "Training's a wrap." I patted both men on the arms and turned for the door.

Sato stepped to block my exit. "The Enclave won't allow it."

"Allow it?" I laughed. "I think you misunderstand. I'm not asking for their permission. I'm telling you what is going to happen."

Sato didn't budge, and I tried to think of a way around him that didn't end up with one of us hurt. Probably me. I opened the valve and let a little more demon power fill me. Based on the way Sato stared at my eyes, I was betting they had turned black.

Yessss, Raum hissed. He sent me the image of a headless demon who must have been among his kills.

"Stop," Aleksei commanded.

I ignored him, drawing even more power through the bond. Sato dropped into a fighter's stance, eyes glinting with something dangerous at the challenge he saw in mine.

Aleksei stepped between us. "I might have a workaround."

I waited for his explanation, while Sato stayed primed for

a fight and Raum pouted at once again being denied an outlet for his bloodlust.

"Follow me."

For Aleksei, Sato stood down. I dialed back the demon power and followed them out of the courtyard. A few minutes later, we were all huddled in the communications room waiting for Aleksei's video call to connect. It didn't take long. The other Volkov joined the call from Kansas City with Craig at his side.

Max Volkov wore his usual dour expression. "What do you want? I have things to do."

Aleksei frowned at his brother. "You didn't find the goat shifter, did you?"

Max Volkov raked a hand through his already disheveled hair. "I'm working on it." Normally, I would have snarked back at him, but it was plain to see he was as worried about Riley as I was.

After explaining the situation, Aleksei proposed his solution. "The only way the Enclave will allow Kali to leave these facilities is if someone capable assumes responsibility for her training."

Craig didn't hesitate. "Done."

"It's not just combat skills she'll need," Aleksei clarified. He grabbed my training weapon from where he'd dropped it on the table and held it up like a prop. "She needs to be able to fight efficiently enough with a war scythe to kill Beleth."

Max Volkov leaned closer to the monitor and squinted. "Are those baby chickens?"

Aleksei dropped the weapon as if burned, and it clattered to the floor. I guessed he'd forgotten about the washi tape when he'd grabbed it for show-and-tell. "Not the point. As I recall, you have some skill with weapons like this, Max."

"I do."

"If you both agree, I believe we can convince the Enclave to entrust her training to the two of you," Aleksei proposed.

"Done," Craig spoke for both of them.

"I'll be on the first flight I can get," I said.

Aleksei frowned. "I need to get the Enclave's sign-off before you can leave."

I wanted to leave immediately, but I wasn't going to push my luck. "Fine. I'll be home soon." It was better than I had expected, but I still worried about the possibility of Masterson going after Drew before I could get there. "In the meantime, can you make sure to spread the word that I'll be coming home? Hopefully, it'll get back to Masterson and dissuade him from going after Drew in the meantime. Now that he's turned an alpha, I'm afraid of what he's capable of." *Could a highly trained Shadow win a fight against one of Masterson's hybrids? Maybe. More than one? Not likely.*

"I'll have the pack spread the word," Max promised.

Craig caught my eye. "I'll head to Chicago and watch out for your family. I can be there in a couple hours."

I choked up, and it took me a minute to get a handle on my emotions. "Thank you," I managed. I turned to Aleksei. "Make the flight to Chicago. I'll meet Craig there." I had to see for myself that Drew and Dad were okay.

Aleksei agreed and disconnected the call.

"I'll take care of the Enclave," Sato said.

Aleksei didn't argue. With nothing left to say, we dispersed. Sato headed back to his room to pack. Aleksei took one look at Sato's retreating back and went in search of another sparring partner. That left me to say my goodbyes to Liv and the others.

Because both Liv and I sucked at the whole goodbye thing,

we kept it short and tear-free. Since her aunt lived in Kansas City, we made plans to get together the next time she was in town, although she did make me promise paintball would not be part of our reunion.

When I finished with my goodbyes, I joined Aleksei, and we stood side by side in the courtyard. Although I had often resented Aleksei's training methods, I was grateful for the results. I was leaving with far better control over my demon bond than I had hoped for.

I bumped him with my shoulder. "Thank you."

He looked down at me, the flash of his wolf just below the surface. "I hope it's enough."

It's going to have to be. Ready or not, I was headed home.

Aleksei stared as Sato and I said our goodbyes. As he watched Sato walk away, I saw the flash of regret before he hid it again.

"Does he know?" I asked softly. With the din of fighting surrounding us, I was confident no one would overhear.

Aleksei stilled but didn't answer, which was answer enough.

"I see the way you watch him when he's not looking." I tilted my head to study him. "Like you are now."

Aleksei glanced at me, and I could see the wolf stirring. "You're more observant than I give you credit for, *ptichka.*"

"Watch it. That was a borderline compliment." I nudged him with my shoulder again. "Why aren't you together?"

He stiffened, watching Sato as he made his way through the throng of people there for his send-off. "It's complicated."

"All the things worth fighting for are." When he didn't respond, I gathered my weapon and sweatshirt and went back to my room to pack, leaving him to say his goodbyes.

I packed up my belongings and stacked everything next to

the door for my early departure in the morning. In a matter of a few short weeks, this place had changed me. Only time would tell if it would be enough. I'd come seeking a way to shut myself off from the demon inhabiting my body, but I was leaving with the knowledge that Raum was an inextricable part of me. Aleksei had taught me that much.

In the morning, the only trace of me left would be the wild dogs who now roamed the halls, the glitter pens I wrapped and labeled for Liv, and the leftover washi tape I left for Aleksei to find in his desk drawer after I was gone.

CHAPTER 16

Unlike his brother who loved his chartered flights, Aleksei was perfectly content to bundle me onto a commercial flight for Chicago. I spent most of the flight considering what I'd say to Craig when I saw him—whether I'd address the potential landmine in our relationship or not. When the plane landed hours later, I still had no idea whether I'd ask him if he'd been the Shadow assigned to carry out my kill order when we'd met. I was certain he'd tell me the truth. What I didn't know was whether I could bear it.

Craig met me at the airport, dressed in his trademark broken-in blue jeans and snug black t-shirt. With his height and build, he was easy to spot as he scanned the passengers filing off the plane. As soon as I met his eyes, all that mattered was getting to his arms. I dropped my bags on the floor next to him and wrapped myself around him, ignoring the amused looks of the people near us. His lips crashed into mine, and for the first time in weeks, I was home.

By the time he'd set me back on my feet, I'd made up my mind. I didn't care how we started. I might not walk away from the showdown with Masterson, and I didn't want to waste a moment fighting with the man I loved over something that couldn't be changed. If I got through what was coming for me, then I could worry about confronting our origins.

Craig picked my carryon bag off the floor and slid the strap over his shoulder. We walked hand in hand through the airport to the baggage claim area. Craig raised a brow after he pulled the third suitcase full of costumes off the conveyor, but he didn't complain. After we loaded everything into his rental car, we headed for the neighborhood I grew up in. I needed to see for myself that my dad and brother were okay.

"Any sign of Masterson?" I asked as we drove.

"None." Craig merged into traffic. "I've been tailing your brother. He's a man of routine."

"Meaning predictable," I ventured.

"Yes. According to reports, he goes to his gym every day at the same time."

"Reports?" I asked.

"I called in some favors to get eyes on him as soon as you told me he was a target," Craig said.

"Thank you," I whispered.

He reached over and squeezed my hand. "Apparently, Drew doesn't vary his route or the time by more than a few minutes. When he's done, he goes straight home." He frowned. "He's an attacker's dream. Same thing, same time, every day."

My brother Drew was a big guy and a cop. Those two things gave him a false sense of security. He had never felt the need to look over his shoulder or avoid the dark alleys like I had. And that made him complacent. He had no concept of being prey in the world he knew. Unfortunately, the real world was brimming with bigger, badder predators than he could imagine.

"He's an easy target for Masterson," I concluded.

"Yeah. I've been following him everywhere, and he's had no clue I was there." Craig shook his head as if he couldn't fathom someone being that oblivious of the danger tracking him. "You'd think he'd be a little more aware of his surroundings." Whether it was the gargoyle in him or the lessons drilled into him at the Compound, Craig never let his guard down enough for someone to get the jump on him. Clearly, he was having difficulty understanding how someone with Drew's background could be so careless.

"I'll talk to him," I said, even knowing that it would likely go over about as well as Drew lecturing me about my fashion sense.

I spent the rest of the drive to my dad's giving Craig a crash course in demon history, including listing the various artifacts hidden in our world. I saved the mood-killer of a prophecy tucked into my bra, figuring that was a discussion for later. Right now, I needed to focus on how I was going to get my pig-headed brother to realize he was just as vulnerable as the rest of us.

Craig parked the rental car behind Drew's in the driveway, effectively blocking his only means of escape. The last time the four of us had been in the same house, my brother stormed out after hurling insults at both Craig and me. Even after the horrible way Drew had treated him, Craig hadn't hesitated to call in favors and come here himself to keep him safe. I leaned over the center console and grabbed his shirt, tugging him closer for a kiss.

"Thank you," I said again, leaning my forehead against his.

"You don't have to thank me, Kali. I'll protect your family

like they're my own." He nipped at my bottom lip. "Even your asshole brother."

I chuckled and kissed him again. Then, I gathered my courage and climbed out of the car. I'd called Dad from the airport in Romania, so he was expecting us. He thought we were in town for yet another of Craig's security consulting gigs. Because he had no idea Craig or I were anything other than human, it was the most logical excuse I could come up with.

My dad met us at the door with a bright smile for both of us. At least that was an improvement over our last visit. He shook Craig's hand and then held the door open for us.

Drew was camped out on the living room couch, his scowl far less welcoming. Dad shot him a dirty look. Reluctantly, he stood up to shake Craig's hand.

"Did you just get in?" Drew asked in an attempt at polite conversation.

"Straight from the airport," Craig said, not mentioning the time he'd spent in Chicago before I'd arrived.

We all sat down and made small talk while I waited for an opening and tried to figure out the best way to bring up my warning. It came sooner than I expected.

"What kind of security work brings you back to Chicago?" Drew practically spat the word "security." He still held onto his belief that Craig's security work was a smokescreen for some kind of nefarious criminal behavior.

I fought the urge to roll my eyes.

Craig beat me to an explanation. "Actually, that's one of the reasons we stopped."

All three of us looked at him curiously. We hadn't talked about this on the way over, so I had no idea how he was going to play this.

"I'm consulting on a cop killer case."

Dad sat up straighter in his chair. "Oh?" He looked at Drew. "I haven't heard anything about a case like that. Have you?"

Drew shook his head. "Who'd you say you are working for?"

"I didn't." Craig said.

"If there was a cop killer case open, I'd know about it," Drew bit out.

"Not if it was a federal case." Craig met his eyes.

Smart man. Craig didn't say it was a federal case, but the implication was enough for my brother to bite. There was nothing that set my brother on edge more than the thought of the feds muscling in on a local issue and keeping the Chicago PD in the dark.

Drew scowled.

"The killer has killed before, including a cop in Kansas City," Craig said.

"A serial killer?" Dad asked.

"It appears so," Craig said. "He targets mid-career officers —usually vice—and follows them, learning their routines and routes. Then, he waits for an opportunity to ambush them. It looks like they never see it coming." Craig was careful to keep his attention on Dad, so Drew could come to his own conclusions. "The working theory is that the killer is someone looking for retribution."

Dad scratched his cheek. "You think it's someone with a record?"

"Maybe," Craig conceded. "Or maybe someone looking for a little payback for a loved one."

Dad nodded. "That fits."

"Anyway," Craig said. "The feds are keeping this quiet." He

waited until Drew was bristling with anger before hitting him with the warning. He looked at my brother. "I thought you deserved to know. Spread the word to your guys to keep their eyes open. Vary your routes and don't get complacent. A bullet shot from a dark alley will take out even the most seasoned cop."

Drew nodded. "I'll make sure to get the word out."

"And you watch your back, as well," I added.

Drew's serious facade slipped, and I got a glimpse of the brother I had grown up with. "You worried about me, kiddo?"

"Always." My voice cracked despite my smile, giving away my fear for him.

"Hey," he said, pulling me up from the couch and into a bear hug. "I'll be careful."

"Good." I punched him playfully in the side. Unlike our normal roughhousing, this time, I had to pull my punch.

Now that Drew and Craig had a shared distrust of the feds to bond them, the rest of our visit was far more pleasant than our last. One look at the sad state of my dad's refrigerator, and we all voted to go out for dinner. The nostalgia of hot dogs with all the fixings won out over fine dining. Although my brother and Craig didn't end the evening as friends, Drew's sniping had moved into good-natured ribbing terri-tory instead of drawing-first-blood insults. I was calling it a win.

Craig's phone rang on the way to the hotel for the night. "Ward," he answered, all business. I couldn't hear the other end of the conversation, but it was impossible to miss the relief on Craig's face as he listened. "Thanks, man. I'll let her know."

He hung up and turned a hundred-watt smile on me. "That was Max. Riley's back, safe and sound."

I slumped against the seat. "Oh, thank God. Where was she?"

Craig shrugged. "He didn't say. You can grill her when we get home tomorrow."

"Damn right, I will." She'd scared me half to death with her little disappearing act. Going off grid like that wasn't like her, and I needed to know what had prompted it.

I waited until we got back to the hotel to spring the prophecy on Craig. Even though I would've much rather spent the time wrapped around each other in that king-sized bed, there was too much at stake to keep him in the dark about this.

After reading the prophecy to him, he took the paper from my hands to study it for himself. I knew what he was doing. It was the same thing I did every time I read it myself—looking for a loophole, a way for this to all end with a happily-ever-after. Ten minutes of staring at it didn't give him the answers he was looking for, though, and he handed the paper back to me.

"Demons can't be trusted." He pointed to the paper in my hand. "It could be lies, for all we know."

"It could be," I conceded, even though I knew better. The words rang true to me every time I read them. "But whether it's the truth or lies, we need to find those weapons. With Beleth's strength, they are the only things that can take out Masterson."

"Agreed. Run through what you know about the scythe and the dagger, again."

"Both were forged in hellfire, and both are hidden some-where in this world," I said dryly.

Craig ran a hand over the back of his neck. "That's not a lot to go on."

"No. It's not." I dug around in my carryon until I came up with the scrying orb. "But I do have this."

"What is it?" he asked.

"I think it's our ticket to finding demon artifacts." Hopefully, now that we were away from the Compound and Sato's watchful gaze, Raum could help me figure out how to use it to locate the artifacts sooner rather than later. If Masterson got his hands on those weapons before we did, we were all screwed.

"Hey. We'll figure it out." Craig took the orb out of my hands and set it on the hotel dresser. "But not tonight."

He sat on the edge of the bed to take off his shoes. His shirt came off next, his eyes on mine as he pulled it over his head. Even in human form, Craig was packed with muscle. Him sitting on the edge of the bed in nothing but blue jeans chased every thought out of my head except for him.

He held out a hand. "Come here. Let me see you."

I stepped closer and took his hand. He pulled me to him until I was standing between his thighs. Craig may have stoicism down to an art form, but I'd never seen eyes as expressive as the slate gray ones drinking me in. And right now, they shone bright with emotion. "I don't ever want to spend that long away from you again," he said.

"I've missed you, too," I whispered.

His smile was wicked. "Show me."

I pushed him back on the bed and did just that.

CHAPTER 17

All I wanted when I got home was to spend the next week sewing in the comfort of my shop and binge-watching bad eighties movies with my friends. Unfortunately, all I had time to do was drop my luggage off at my apartment, check in with Emma to make sure everything was running smoothly, and take a quick shower before heading to Volkov's for my welcome-back Tribunal meeting.

Craig knocked on the door as I was tucking the scrying orb into my favorite sling bag. It was a fun Halloween print with dancing skeletons on it. I bought it before it held any irony for me, and I refused to stop using it just because my life had turned into an undead shitshow.

"Riley's coming, right?" I asked as we drove over to Volkov's house. Craig had already told me she was, but I wanted the reassurance.

"Already there."

We were the last to arrive. The vampire seat on the Tribunal had yet to be filled after I lit the previous occupant on fire. That left Max Volkov, Meira, and Celeste as the governing members.

While Celeste and Volkov both greeted me, Meira's reception was frostier. She looked pointedly between Volkov, Craig, and me. "I assume we can dispense with the cloak and dagger routine now, and you can brief Celeste and me on where you've been?"

When I'd decided to train with Aleksei, I'd purposely kept that information from the group at large. Only Volkov, Craig, and Riley knew where I'd gone. We'd told the others that Volkov had a connection who specialized in helping raging shifters get control over their beasts. That much had been true. However, we hadn't mentioned that the connection happened to be his brother or that I'd be training at the Compound. Although my past suspicions about Meira and the witches' council had proven unfounded, I'd heeded the instinct that urged me to guard my location closely as I got a handle on my new demon bond. From the expressions on both women's faces, they resented being left out of the loop.

Before I could unruffle their feathers, Riley provided a welcome distraction. She launched herself out of the chair she was draped across as soon as she spotted me. She collided with me, and I was glad I'd put the orb in the sling bag across my back. The demon orb might have housed hellfire, but it still seemed breakable to me.

I hugged Riley back. "You scared the crap out of me," I accused once she let go.

"I'm sorry."

I ignored everyone else in the room, anxious to make sure she was okay. "Where were you?"

"Yeah, about that." She glanced at Volkov, who was

scowling at her from across the room. "We may have a slight problem."

Despite the Tribunal members who stood dour faced around us, I couldn't help but laugh. That was the understatement of the year. "I think I may have you beat."

She hooked an arm over my shoulder and tugged me toward the couch. Everyone watched as we sat down. Riley tucked a leg beneath her and turned toward me. "Do you remember that dagger Zepar told me about?"

I frowned. "The one you thought about stealing?"

Volkov cleared his throat and glared at her.

"That's the one," she said brightly. "I took it."

"Stole it," Volkov corrected.

She waved a hand dismissively. "Whatever. You should have seen it, Kali. It was a thing of beauty. This long," she said, holding her hands to indicate the dagger length, "and made of steel so shiny, I could see myself in it. The handle was tipped with a pentagram, and next to the blade were these crescent moons facing outward with a stone in the center. It was incredible. I swear, I could see flames when I looked into that stone."

I stilled, my throat closing in fear as her description called up an image I'd seen on the pages of the demon volumes at the Enclave.

"Do you have it?" I whispered.

She shook her head. "I hid it right after I took it, but I went back for it when a buyer contacted me." Riley paled. "When I went to meet the buyer, something felt off."

"What do you mean?" Craig asked.

"At first, it was just a feeling. But right before our meet time, a big black van pulled up, and the driver was wearing shades even though it was cloudy out." Riley shrugged. "I took off."

"Smart girl," Craig said, and the others nodded.

"Not so much." Riley looked at Volkov, who was clenching his jaw hard enough to crack walnuts. "I ran straight into a guy I recognized."

Even though I knew exactly who it was, I needed to hear her say it. "Who?"

"That nerdy guy who rented the shop next to yours," Riley said. "Frederick Masterson."

Craig swore. "He took the dagger?"

Riley looked miserable as she nodded.

"What's going on?" Volkov demanded.

"I'd say we have more than a slight problem." Although Craig had given the Tribunal a rundown of the basics after our video call while I was at the Compound, I filled in the gaps. "Masterson, and, more importantly, Beleth, is now in possession of one of two weapons capable of killing demons."

Riley ran a hand through her hair. "Well, shit."

"Why do we care if Beleth wants to kill demons?" Celeste asked.

It was a good question. The answer was an ugly one. "Because he'll use our world as a battleground to do it. He's already raising his army to position himself to take back his throne. To get there, he'll have to go through a lot of demons, including the vampires loyal to the other kings." The Enclave representative and I had spent many hours hashing through what we knew in order to come up with our working theory of what Beleth wanted. "In the hell dimension, Beleth won't stand a chance against the five remaining demon kings. Even with the dagger, it wouldn't be enough to defeat all the legions of demons the other kings command."

"Then, what does it matter?" Meira asked. "Let him have the dagger."

"You don't get it," I snapped. "The dagger is just the first step. He'll go after the other artifacts next—the scythe and the shield, the book of dark magic spells, a black fire tourmaline crystal." I reached into my bag and pulled out the scrying orb. "And this orb."

Meira stared at the flames in fascination, bending closer for a better look.

Volkov asked the question everyone was likely thinking. "Why?"

"Because once he has those artifacts, he'll lure the other demon kings here, one by one, so that he can kill them. Once they're dead, there will be no one to stand between him and the throne he sees as stolen from him. But in the meantime, our world will be a war zone."

I let the stark reality of what that meant sink in. Craig and Volkov got it first. Then, Celeste and Riley blanched.

Meira reached out and touched the orb, pulling back as if the flames within it burnt her hand. "Then, I guess we'd better get to the other artifacts before he does." She looked to me. "How does this work?"

I sighed. "I'm still working on that part."

Celeste reached for it. "May I?"

I handed her the scrying orb. She turned it so she could examine it from every angle, watching as the flame danced inside the glass. "What is this?" she asked, awe in her voice.

"Hellfire," I said.

Celeste fumbled the orb before handing it back to me. "What have you tried so far when scrying?"

I explained my attempt back at the Compound. Since then, I hadn't had a lot of time to experiment.

Celeste walked over to Volkov's well-stocked bookcases. Finding the book she was looking for, she set it on the library table and flipped through the pages. "I don't know if demon orbs work the same as regular scrying orbs, but according to this, it's the intention that determines how successful the practitioner will be in pulling forth an image."

"What does that even mean?" Riley asked.

"It means you need to be very, very specific about what you ask to see," Celeste said.

Meira picked up the book but didn't read the pages. Instead, she seemed to be thinking it through. "You've seen drawings of these artifacts?" she asked me.

"Yes, and Raum has shown me the weapons in action."

"Good. Close your eyes and picture one of them, then try to scry its location from the orb." She watched me expectantly.

"Now?"

"Yes, Kali. Now." She set the book back down with a thump. "Let's start with the shield."

"Why the shield?" Craig challenged. "Kali has more need of the scythe to protect herself and to kill Beleth."

"That may be," Meira conceded. "But Beleth is going to go after the shield next. He already has a weapon capable of killing demons."

Craig's jaw tightened, but I squeezed his hand in reassurance. "She's right. We should start with the shield."

I tried to picture the shield in my head, but it was hard to concentrate with everyone watching me. "Is there somewhere less crowded I can do this?"

"Follow me," Volkov said.

"I'll go with you," Meira offered.

"Thanks, but I really need to be alone to focus."

Meira didn't look thrilled about staying on the sidelines. I suspected she was still irritated at being kept in the dark about my trip to the Compound.

Volkov led me to the living room off the main entrance. While I'd been in his house plenty of times, I usually stuck to the library. This was the room where I'd confronted him about being a werewolf and saw my life flash in front of my eyes when he'd wrapped his hand around my neck. From the look on his face, he was remembering the same incident.

I stared at him, an uncomfortable thought rising to the surface. *If he was the Shadow, wouldn't he have already known that I was a necromancer back then?* Volkov was a lot of things, but a skilled actor didn't seem to be one of them. With him, what you saw was what you got. I pushed the thought back down.

"Thanks," I mumbled as he left me alone.

Okay, give me some pointers, buddy, I told Raum.

My crow tattoo undulated as Raum answered. *Picture the weapon you want to find and then ask the orb to show it to you.*

Really helpful, I snarked.

Raum sighed dramatically. *The key is to keep focusing on it once the orb shows you what you seek. The longer you see it, the more details you'll notice about where it's hidden.*

I got comfortable, sitting in the middle of the plush carpet and closing my eyes. I recalled the illustration of the shield, then revisited the image of it from Raum's visions. When I was sure I had it, I opened my eyes and picked up the orb again. This time, when I looked into the flames, they flared out, showing me the shield in the center of the flames. My heart began racing, but I forced myself to remain still—to keep looking. It wasn't enough to see the shield. I needed to know where to find it.

I concentrated. Then, I willed the image to zoom out. It took a long time, but eventually, it worked. I could see the space where the shield was located. It was hanging, like a decoration, on an otherwise blank wall.

If it weren't for the dent in the wall directly below the shield, the wall would have looked like any other. But this divot I recognized from when I'd stared at it to avoid looking at a table full of vamps ready to toast with my blood.

I felt Raum's triumph at locating the shield through our bond. *Alright, one down. Let's try two for two,* I thought. I closed my eyes again, this time concentrating on the image of the war scythe.

It took me several tries, but eventually, the flame showed me what I sought. Now that I'd had some practice navigating a scrying vision, it was easier for me to refocus the image. Once I had a broader view, I made note of anything that might give away the war scythe's location.

This time, it wasn't a place I recognized. The scythe was in a large glass display case in the middle of a modest-sized room. Against one wall was a line of nondescript filing cabinets like those sold in big-box office stores everywhere. I could see security cameras mounted in the two corners of the room. Both were aimed at the display case that housed the war scythe, along with a few other objects I didn't recognize. One was a pendant that looked antique. Another was an old scroll bound with fraying twine. Runestones were piled next to it.

I scanned the room for any other distinguishing characteristics but came up blank. It wasn't much to go on, but it was the best I could do. I stood abruptly, tucking the scrying orb back into my bag.

Everyone looked up when I entered the library.

"You found it?" Meira asked hopefully.

I nodded. "I saw both the war scythe and the shield."

"They're together?" Meira asked incredulously.

"No." I looked around the room at their expectant faces. "They're in two different locations." I took a steadying breath.

"Well," Volkov snapped. "Did you recognize where they were?"

"One of them." I caught Craig staring at me. He wasn't going to like where. I started with the location I didn't recognize. "But the war scythe was in a small room that looked almost like a bedroom."

Volkov scowled. "That doesn't exactly narrow it down."

Craig glared at him. "If you stop interrupting, Kali might be able to tell us something that will."

Volkov stiffened, but he stayed quiet. Riley smirked at him and held her hand out to Craig for a fist bump. Both men ignored her.

"I don't know if any of what I saw will be helpful in finding it, but here's what I noticed." I described the room, from the carpet to the wall of four-drawer filing cabinets suitable for an accountant's office. I also told them about the security features and the other items in the glass case next to the war scythe.

I'd been so focused on recounting the details, I hadn't noticed how pale Riley had grown until I was finished. All the color had drained from her cheeks, which was all the more noticeable because of her vivid blue eyes and shockingly pink hair.

"What is it?" I asked her.

"I know where it is," she whispered, looking stricken at the knowledge.

We all looked at her. Seeing the blatant fear on her face, Volkov's face darkened. "Where?"

She didn't answer right away. I reached for her hand, but Volkov beat me to her side. He gripped Riley by the shoulders and locked eyes with her. "You've been there before?"

She nodded slowly.

Volkov leaned in. "Wherever it is, you don't have to go there," he assured her. "Just tell me where to find it."

Riley snapped out of it, shaking her head. "He'll put it up for auction."

"Who?" Volkov's voice was threaded with an alpha command, but while the rest of us felt it, it bounced right off Riley.

Her eyes shimmered for a second, and my heart ached for her. "It doesn't matter." She pulled away from Volkov. "We need to find the next supernatural black market auction. That's where it'll be."

Meira perked up. "We'll just buy it."

Volkov glared at her, obviously still angry at whatever had Riley afraid. "If we leave it to an auction, what's to stop Masterson from getting to it first?"

"That would be me," Riley said, sounding more like herself again. "We find the auction location, and I'll steal it out from under his nose."

I didn't know which he she was referring to—Masterson or the mysterious man whose room she recognized from my vision. Either way, it sounded like our best option.

Volkov started to shake his head no, but Riley cut him off. "Are you going to steal it?" She scanned him from the tips of his polished dress shoes to his broad shoulders encased in a tailored business suit. Not only was he ill-prepared for burglary, the sheer size of the man meant there was no way in hell he could sneak in anywhere undetected. I'd never seen his wolf form, but I'd bet good money that it was as massive as the man.

From the look on his face, he knew it, too. "Fine, but I'm going with you."

"Fine," Riley snarked back at him.

She might have been throwing attitude about his insistence on going, but I couldn't help but notice the tension ease from her shoulders when she agreed.

While the two of them glared at each other, everyone else looked back to me.

"What about the shield?" Meira asked. "Do you know where it is?"

"I do." I braced for Craig's reaction. "Hanging in Wallace Ratcliff's formal dining room."

I expected him to scowl, so I was shocked when he smiled instead. "Good. I've been meaning to pay the master vampire a visit." Craig was still furious Ratcliff had attacked me the last time we'd met up.

"Ward," Volkov warned.

Craig wasn't in the mood to listen. He glanced at Riley and then back to Volkov. "You worry about your business, and I'll handle mine." He stepped closer. Volkov didn't back down.

Riley and I rolled our eyes at the same time. "You want to grab barbecue and plan our heists?" she asked.

"Hell yeah." I snagged Craig's keys from his pocket. "We'll be back in a couple hours," I called over my shoulder as Riley and I left them to it.

CHAPTER 18

There was no question that Riley's love language was smoked meats smothered in sweet barbecue sauce. She popped the last of her sandwich in her mouth and moaned, oblivious to the businessmen at the table next to us who kept darting glances her way. I'd missed the unfiltered enthusiasm with which this girl did absolutely everything.

When she looked at her now empty plate with sadness, I slid my half-finished sandwich across the table to her as I filled her in on the last few weeks of my life.

I waited until she polished off the last of my brisket before getting down to business. "Are you going to tell me who has the war scythe?"

Riley glanced around the barbecue joint. Once she was satisfied no one was listening, she answered. "The room you described matched one I've seen before." She waited until an older couple passed by our table on the way to the restrooms in the back.

"Who did the room belong to?" I prodded.

She dropped her voice so low that I had to strain to hear

her. "The vampire who runs the North American supernatural black market auctions."

I narrowed my eyes. "Are you telling me you were involved in black market auctions?" Although I had no idea what such auctions entailed, I was betting it was a dangerous business.

"I wouldn't say I was involved with the auctions," Riley hedged.

"Then how did you recognize the room?"

She wiped her mouth with her napkin and tossed it on her empty plate. "The last job Carl had me do was to rob that vampire." Carl was the alpha of the Santa Fe pack Riley had lived with after her parents' deaths. He'd molded her into a world-class thief and then forced her to steal for him.

I rubbed my temples. If being involved with black market auctions was dangerous, ripping off the man in charge of them was a suicide mission. "And you got away with it?"

She grinned. "Of course."

I didn't return her smile. "This is a bad idea. Trying to rob him twice is just begging to get caught."

"Oh, relax." She shrugged off my concern. "That was years ago. Besides, he had no idea who was responsible for the theft."

"You're sure?" I asked.

"Positive."

I didn't like the idea of her hitting him twice, but I had to have that war scythe. "This vamp is in Santa Fe, I take it?"

Riley took a long drink of her water before answering me. "Maybe. That's where he lives, but he's rich as hell. He probably has fancy-ass vacation homes all over. Depending on where the next auction will be held, he could be anywhere."

I stared at her. That didn't exactly narrow it down.

"I've still got a couple connections in that world. I'll get the location of the next auction and go from there." She flagged down the waitress to get us refills.

Once the waitress was gone again, Riley changed the subject before I could continue my line of questioning. "How are you planning on getting into Ratcliff's mansion to get the shield, anyway?"

I took a sip of my recently topped off drink and shrugged. "I figured I'd just knock on Ratcliff's door."

Riley laughed, but when I kept a straight face, her laugh faltered. "Yeah, that's not gonna work."

"It might. If we have the Enclave's backing and a group of Aleksei's men with us, Ratcliff would be forced to hand it over," I reasoned.

"You sure the Enclave will have your back?" she challenged.

I wanted to brush off her question, but doubts lingered. "It's in their best interest to back me on this."

Riley grimaced. "It may be in their best interest for you to take it, but trust me, that doesn't mean they'll put their neck on the line while you go after it." Her voice was tinged with bitterness. "To people like them, you're just another tool in their arsenal."

I reached across the table and squeezed her hand, but I couldn't argue her point. "Either way, we'll get it." I'd ask Aleksei to send the request through and go from there. She might well have been right, but there was no sense in borrowing trouble as my grandma used to say. At the thought of her, an unexpected pang of grief hit, but I brushed it aside.

Riley leaned in. "You know, I could steal it for you."

"No way." Stealing an artifact from an auction organizer was one thing. Sneaking into a house full of vampires to get the shield was another. "Ratcliff's mansion is teeming with vampires. There's no way you'd get in and out alive."

She clutched her heart like I'd mortally wounded her. "I like my odds."

I laughed. "No one likes those odds."

Our conversation drifted to lighter fare, starting with a play-by-play account of the Helen vs. Aleksei showdown. By the time we left the restaurant, we were both laughing.

Riley made a couple of calls on the way back to Volkov's house. She finally got ahold of her black market auction contact, but it was apparent even from the one-sided conversation I could hear that he was skittish. It didn't surprise me when she told me he insisted on meeting her in person before sharing intel.

By the time Riley and I made it back to Volkov's, I was relieved to see Meira and Celeste were long gone. That left the four of us to plan our next moves. I lobbied hard for getting right back on a plane bound for Bucharest. Craig convinced me to wait a couple days before returning. Our odds of successfully walking out of Ratcliff's home with the shield depended on the element of surprise. Unfortunately, secrecy was something that required time and resources. Since neither of us wanted a repeat of our trip that led Masterson straight to Naomi, we needed to make sure our trip would be under the radar.

Unlike the waiting game the rest of us were playing, Riley planned to leave in the dead of night to meet her contact alone. Riley's contact was someone who made a living trading information about supernatural power players. According to Riley, his survival depended on keeping his identity a closely guarded secret. Since nothing sent informants to ground faster than spotting an authority figure lurking in the background, Volkov reluctantly agreed to catch up with Riley post-meeting.

I didn't like letting Riley go off on her own to meet some shady contact any more than Volkov did, but despite my fear for her, I trusted her when she said it was the only way. I hugged her before she left. "Any sign of trouble," I reminded her.

"I hightail it out there," she finished.

Rather than going home to wait for Riley's return, Craig, Volkov, and I camped out in Volkov's living room with cheap pizza and expensive craft beer. My suggestion of playing a board game had been met with stony silence, so I settled for flipping through the channels on Volkov's monstrosity of a television until I found a suitably mindless reality show to help pass the time.

Two and a half hours after she left, Riley was back with the coordinates of the next black market auction in three days' time. With Riley's piece of the plan in motion, it was time to go after the shield.

My phone rang as Craig and I were headed home. Craig pulled over, and I put Aleksei's call on speaker. It didn't take long for the Enclave to prove Riley right. "You've got to be kidding me," I said.

"They can't afford to appear directly involved with this." Even Aleksei sounded frustrated, but like a good soldier, he wouldn't go against the Enclave's directive.

"In case I fail."

Aleksei's answering silence was confirmation enough. I hung up and turned to Craig, who looked like he was ready to take some heads off.

"One of these days, I'm actually going to get to try a Plan A," I joked, trying to ease some of the tension riding us both.

Craig stared out his window for several minutes, fists clenched and jaw tight. When he turned toward me, he was back in control. "If I go in alone, I can bargain with Ratcliff," he reasoned.

I was shaking my head before he finished. "I'm going." I crossed my arms. "Let's skip the part where you try to keep me out of the fray and come up with a plan that might actually work."

Craig hooked a hand around my bicep and pulled me across the seat until I was tucked against his side. "Alright. We'll come up with a plan together."

In the end, we decided to go the simple route. We'd ask Ratcliff for it.

CHAPTER 19

Wallace Ratcliff's home was a lot like the vampire himself—old, hauntingly beautiful, and full of decay. The mansion was a large stone structure nestled on an oversized lot in Bucharest. The grounds around the mansion were untended, nature crowding into every crack or crevice it could take root in.

The last time I'd paid a visit to Ratcliff, I had been on the dinner menu. If it hadn't been for Aleksei's intervention, I might still be chained in the medieval dungeon I was certain a man like Ratcliff kept well-equipped for guests. I fought back the shudder that raced through me at the thought.

Craig looked up at the darkening sky and then back to me. "You ready?"

"As ready as I'll ever be." I reached for my bond with Raum, drawing enough strength from him to ensure I was battle ready. Although my throwing knives were strapped to my thighs, something Craig had insisted on, the demon bonded to me was the only weapon that stood a chance in a seethe of vampires.

We'd debated waiting to confront Ratcliff until I had the war scythe in hand, but we didn't have the time to spare. We didn't want to risk Masterson getting wind of us going after one of the artifacts and beat us to the other. It was bad enough he had the dagger. Masterson could strike any day now, and we had to be ready when he did. That meant meeting Ratcliff without the benefit of a weapon that could cut through vampires like butter.

Only weak demons are content to be blood drinkers, Raum said. *They are no match for Raum the Almighty.*

We talked about this. No way am I calling you that. Now simmer down until I need you, I told him.

You do need me, girl. Don't forget it.

I ignored him until he settled.

Because we didn't want to risk Ratcliff not being in residence when we paid him a visit, we had made an appointment. Aleksei arranging this meeting was the full extent of his help, though, so from here on out, we were on our own.

Even though we were here to try to reason with the master vampire, things had a way of going sideways fast when it came to Ratcliff. That was why as soon as we stepped foot onto Ratcliff's land, Craig shifted to his gargoyle form. He grew to over seven feet tall, with skin as gray and impenetrable as stone. He folded his mighty wings behind him and bared his teeth as we walked toward Ratcliff's mansion. Between the gargoyle at my side and the demon attached to my soul, I hoped it would be enough to walk out of here with the shield.

One of Ratcliff's lackeys met us at the front door, saving us from knocking. "This way." He led the way deeper into Ratcliff's domain.

Ratcliff was a man who appreciated theatrics. His

vampires filled the home like creepy mannequins. In the living room, they sat perfectly still on couches and wingback chairs, only their eyes moving as they tracked us. They lined the hallways like undead sentinels. I expected our tour guide to lead us to the formal dining room for Act II of Ratcliff's little dinner theater show. Instead, he passed the room without a glance.

I resisted the urge to dart inside for a snatch-and-grab instead of playing this out. Craig nudged me as if reading my mind, and I kept walking.

We stopped at a closed door that turned out to be to Ratcliff's office. Inside, vampires lined the wall behind Ratcliff, their faces blank. Ratcliff rose from his chair like a gracious host to greet us.

Nothing about Ratcliff's appearance was threatening. With his trim build, messy golden blonde hair, and elegant attire, he appeared both young and charming—neither of which he actually was. He ignored Craig and stared at me, animosity twisting his otherwise angelic features. Nothing of that animosity could be detected in his cordial greeting, though. "Welcome to my home."

Everything in me wanted to antagonize this man, poke at his weak spots, but I tamped the urge down. When he took a step around his desk to come closer, Craig growled a warning, the sound rumbling through the room. Ratcliff's gaze darted between us. I didn't like the calculating gleam in his eyes as he put his desk between us again and gestured for us to take our seats.

I sat in the closest chair.

Craig made no move toward the remaining chair, taking up a position at my back instead. "I'll stand."

Ratcliff didn't object. He turned his full attention to me.

"I'm surprised you had the courage to walk back in here, little girl."

You are the destroyer, and he should tremble at your feet, Raum boomed inside my head. For once, we were in agreement.

I pulled a little more power, letting the demon shine through my eyes as I looked back at him. "I'm full of surprises."

Ratcliff's jaw tightened. He got right to the point. "What is it you want?"

I indicated the vampires lining the wall like props. "This conversation isn't one for an audience."

"Surely, you can't expect me to be stupid enough to meet with the two of you alone," he scoffed.

"Do you really think a few vampires would save you if I wanted you dead?" Craig crowded my back as he spoke. "Keep whoever you are certain are loyal to you. What we have to say, you won't want to go past these walls."

Ratcliff dismissed the room with a tilt of his head. Only two of the vampires remained in the room with us, taking up positions flanking Ratcliff.

When the room was clear, I reached in my bag and pulled out four small stones. Ratcliff watched as I placed one stone in front of the closed door and the others against each wall of the room. When the stones were in place, I read the incantation Celeste had given me to activate the silencing spell. Once enacted, anything we said wouldn't travel beyond the perimeter of the stones.

Satisfied we had our privacy, I took my seat again. Ratcliff kept his expression neutral, but I knew from the way he leaned forward that he was curious about what had brought us here.

What I was about to do grated on every instinct I had. I

was about to partner with a man I held responsible for my sister's death. Garadin Aldea may have been the one who killed Claire, but I had no doubt that he had done so on Ratcliff's command. The last person whose help I wanted to enlist was the evil bastard sitting across from me. But sometimes, there wasn't a better choice. I might have hated what I had to do, but I wasn't willing to sacrifice the living for the dead any longer. I'd do what I had to in order to protect my family and friends.

Because Ratcliff wasn't the only one in the room who appreciated theatrics, I started with a performance of my own. Reaching into my pocket, I pulled out my crib sheet and read the words that were now hardwired into my psyche.

Beware the dangers born unto the human world,
twins birthed on the eve of a new moon
with power unlike the world has seen
for they shall be able to call forth demons
and command whole armies of the dead.
When they come, it will be as
the innocent child and the sacrifice,
as the corrupter and the destroyer.
Only the strongest among them shall survive,
two souls bound through magic and bathed in blood,
and the fate of our world shall rest with the victor.

Ratcliff blanched and scrambled to his feet as I read. I refolded the paper and returned it to my pocket. "Good. Then you know who I am."

Destroyer, Raum shouted with glee.

I startled. *Knock it off.* I focused my attention back on Ratcliff, hoping he didn't notice my little jump scare. "Let me tell you why I'm here." I pointed to his chair and waited until he sat back down again. "I'm here to take care of your demon problem once and for all, but I'm going to need your help to do it."

"What kind of help?" he asked warily.

"Since you know all about the prophecy, I take it you also know your demon history."

Ratcliff nodded. He didn't volunteer any details, waiting to see how much I knew.

I obliged, summarizing what I knew about the first demon war and Beleth's dethroning. When I mentioned the hidden demon artifacts, Ratcliff stiffened ever so slightly. *Bingo. He knows what he has hanging in his dining room.* Until that tell, we hadn't been sure whether he knew he was in possession of a demon artifact or if it had been placed under his watch without him knowing what it was.

"Who do you answer to?" I asked. "Beleth?" I watched Ratcliff's reaction closely.

His lip curled into a sneer. "I do not answer to the false king," he spat.

"Let me venture a guess, then. Ashmodai."

The flicker of surprise was as good as a bullseye. Ratcliff stared at me, waiting to see where I was going with this.

I tapped my finger against my cheek. "Of course, since Ashmodai led his legion of war demons to unseat Beleth, that probably puts him at the top of Beleth's hit list."

Ratcliff shrugged. "Why would I concern myself with demon politics?" He gestured to the office around him. "I'm no longer there."

"True," I conceded. "But you have Beleth's shield hanging on your wall, so that tells me you're very much entangled in demon politics."

Ratcliff lunged across the desk, but Craig was ready for him. He had a hand wrapped around the master vampire's throat before Ratcliff came close to me.

"Please," I said, pulling out my polite voice. "Have a seat while we finish our conversation."

Craig shoved him back. The chair hit Ratcliff in the back of his legs, and he sat down.

I furrowed my brow and rubbed my jaw. "I wonder what your demon king would say if he knew you were the one who kicked off the prophecy in the first place," I mused.

Ratcliff paled.

"The innocent child and the sacrifice," I quoted, the accusation heavy in my voice. "Why did you kill my sister?"

Sensing my anger, Raum stirred beneath my skin. *We should take his head and use it to play fetch with our demon rat.* One time of playing fetch with the dogs at the Compound, and Raum turned it into a murder game.

"We thought she was the strongest. Our sources told us she was the key to the prophecy." Ratcliff shrugged as if getting it wrong was of no consequence.

"What sources?" Craig demanded.

Ratcliff sighed. "I didn't ask. Aldea handled it."

At the mention of my sister's killer, the tenuous leash I had on my own demon almost snapped. I took a steadying breath, struggling for a calm I couldn't reach. I pointed my finger at Ratcliff. "By killing her, you are responsible for everything that happened after. If Beleth succeeds, you'll be responsible for that, too. And I will make damn sure Ashmodai knows it was you, even if I have to summon him myself to tell him."

As soon as the words were out of my mouth, I knew they were the truth. Craig jerked in surprise, but he didn't contradict me. Vengeance was a tricky beast, and it rose in me even when I didn't call it. I wanted Ratcliff to answer for what he'd done, and throwing him on the mercy of a bloodthirsty war demon felt a lot like justice at the moment.

Ratcliff stared at me with blatant hatred. "What do you want from me?"

"And the fate of our world shall rest with the victor." I repeated the last line of the prophecy bitterly. "We both know I'm the last one standing, so let me tell you about my vision for the fate of the world because that bit is a little vague. I'm gonna need that shield you have hanging on your wall."

Ratcliff's eyes went red with blood lust as he watched my pulse in my throat. Despite my bravado, it sped up as he bared his fangs.

"Why would I give you the shield?"

I pushed out of my chair and stood to face him. "Because I'm the only chance you've got." I bent down to pick up the stone in front of the door, breaking the spell.

The thing about silencing spells was that they operated both ways. As soon as it was down, the sounds of fighting filtered through the closed door, saving Ratcliff from having to answer.

Craig and I exchanged glances before we all rushed out of the room and into the melee. The closer I got to the fighting, the faster my hopes sank. Craig went first, throwing vampires out of his path like rag dolls.

Despite being outnumbered ten to one, a shifter with the eyes of a demon fought his way through Ratcliff's vampires in the living room, edging closer to the door.

"Shit," I yelled when the man turned to face me. I knew him. He was the shifter chained to the floor in my vision. I called out a warning, so Craig knew what he was dealing with. "He's one of Masterson's—the alpha hybrid."

Craig lunged for him, but several of Masterson's vampires attacked him at the same time, giving the hybrid the time he needed to get to the door. Because the hybrid didn't have the shield, Craig let him go.

I turned away from them. The only thing that mattered was getting to that shield. I pulled so hard on the bond, my vision darkened as I ran for the dining room. Raum was more than happy to oblige. Inside the dining room, a vampire was sprawled across the broken table, his neck twisted at a grotesque angle. Decapitated vampires littered the floor. I sank to my knees among them when I spotted the blank wall where the shield should have hung.

The hybrid had been a distraction, and he hadn't come alone. We were too late.

CHAPTER 20

e left Romania as empty-handed as we had arrived. After landing in Kansas City, we sequestered ourselves in Craig's apartment to regroup. With three international flights in the span of a week, jet lag was kicking my ass. I must have looked as bad as I felt because as soon as we were in the apartment, Craig ushered me off to bed. After a half-hearted protest, I let Craig tuck me under his comforter, so I could sleep it off.

I woke to the delicious scent of fresh blueberry muffins and coffee. It was enough to drag me from beneath the covers. I stumbled bleary-eyed into Craig's kitchen just as he was taking the muffins out of the oven. I examined his handiwork and reached for a muffin.

"Watch out. Those are still hot." He swatted my hand away, shaking his head at my sleep-fuddled state.

"How long have I been asleep?"

Craig pushed me toward a chair. "A few hours. You needed it."

One good look at the assorted baked goods lining his counters was enough to tell me we were screwed. From the muscle packed on Craig's frame, people would have guessed he was one of those men who took his stress out in the weight room or on a punching bag. But the fact was, Craig worked out his stress with a flour sifter and a rolling pin. Based on the state of his kitchen, his stress was off the charts.

I walked around him and turned the oven off before he could start on yeast doughs. I poured us each a cup of coffee and grabbed plates for the muffins. The world might be about to implode, but I'd be damned if muffins that smelled this good went to waste.

He sat but pushed the plate I'd set in front of him away.

"Are Volkov and Riley back yet?" I asked between bites.

"No. I checked in with the pack, and they haven't made it home yet. I also checked with Meira, but she hasn't heard from them."

I pushed the muffin back to him, and this time he ate it. "Masterson would have been focused on the shield since he already had the dagger. Hopefully, that means they will be more successful than we were."

Craig washed down the last of his muffin with a drink of coffee but didn't speculate on their success.

"Even if they do get the scythe, that leaves Masterson with both the dagger and the shield." I stood up and went to the counter. This was definitely a two-muffin kind of day. "Where does that leave us?"

"We need to find his weakness," Craig reasoned.

"Besides the scythe?"

He nodded. "He may be physically vulnerable to the scythe, but that's not the type of weakness I'm talking about."

I frowned. "What, then?"

"Beating an opponent comes down to knowing and exploiting weaknesses. Part of that is physical. If someone favors their right hand over their left or lacks the stamina to take a fight beyond the initial attack, those are all things that can be exploited in a fight. But even more useful than physical weaknesses is knowing the psychological weaknesses." Craig gave me an assessing look, and I was pretty sure I wouldn't like whatever was going to come out of his mouth next. "Like Masterson found yours."

"My sister," I said.

"Your sister," he agreed. "And your friends, your family, and your need for justice."

I finished my coffee, welcoming the jolt of caffeine. "So, we need to find Beleth's weaknesses."

Craig shook his head. "Beleth is the stronger of the two. Masterson is the weak link. We need to find and exploit his weaknesses." Craig talked about finding and exploiting weaknesses with a practiced detachment that came from years as an enforcer and—before that—probably as a Shadow.

Unbidden, I wondered if that was what he'd done with me in those early days. I stood and took our plates to the sink. We had more pressing issues at the moment. That conversation could wait.

"Alright, so here's what we know. Masterson was always power hungry, according to Samara's journals," I said.

When I'd gone looking for Samara's grimoire to figure out how to send Zepar back, I'd stumbled onto her personal journals. In them, she'd written about her lover, Frederick Masterson. Although she had filtered his actions through the rose-colored glasses of a young witch in love, as a reader, it had been easy to see the manipulation. Masterson pushed Samara to summon a demon, and she'd been killed for trying.

"Masterson was always after a demon." I sat back down across from Craig. "So, if he wasn't operating on vengeance for his lover, he was after power."

"That's a start. We need to dig into his past to see what drove him. If we find that, we find his weakness," Craig said.

"The sister," I said as much to myself as to Craig.

"What sister?"

"When I dug into Masterson's background, I discovered he had a sister who died when she was twelve." I thought of Claire and how close we'd been even when we fought. "No one would know his motivations better than she would."

"You want to summon her." He looked dubious. "She's been dead a long time, Kali. Plus, she was twelve when she died. It's possible that the only thing she could tell you about her brother is what kind of toys he liked to play with."

"I have to try."

Craig pushed to his feet. "What do you need?"

"That's the tricky part. I need a conduit—something connected to her." I grimaced. "How do you feel about grave robbing?"

From the genealogical research Alyce had helped me with, I knew where Masterson's sister was buried. Fortunately, she'd been buried on what was now the outskirts of Kansas City, which meant easy access to her grave. All we had to do was wait for the cover of night.

As added insurance, Craig decided to recruit a few of Volkov's shifters to secure a perimeter around the cemetery. I would also enlist Helen's aid to come up with a few surprises. The shifters were good at creating physical barriers, but I didn't want some nosy Nancy watching me dig up a seventy-year-old grave from a third-story apartment window.

Craig and I weren't planning on getting to the cemetery until almost midnight. That gave him plenty of time to make sure the shifters were in position and me the time to finish preparations.

By midmorning, everything was set for a midnight grave robbery save a pit stop at Meira's to pick up some standard necromancer supplies. When I'd called her with our plan, Meira suggested using the candles and spells most necromancers depended on to reach spirits. While I'd never needed such props in the past, I'd also never attempted to raise a spirit from nothing more than old, buried bones. According to Meira, we were lucky that tonight would be a dark moon. She claimed that the phase right before the new moon, when it was a waning crescent, was when the veil was the thinnest. Theoretically, that meant it should make it easier to call upon the spirits. With such a tenuous link, I figured I could use all the power boost I could get.

Because it was a weekend morning, Meira was at home rather than at Old World Occult & Curiosities, where she spent most of her weekdays. She lived in an old farmhouse on the outskirts of the metro, surrounded by wheat fields and gravel roads. After navigating the early morning traffic, I welcomed the quiet found just outside the city limits.

As I turned onto Meira's road, my cell rang, Craig's name flashing on the screen. I pulled over to take the call. "Hello?"

"They got it." No one could accuse the man of burying the lede, and I'd never been so grateful for it.

"Volkov and Riley got the war scythe?"

"Yes. They're about an hour out. They'll meet us at your

place once they hit town. How soon can you get there?" he asked.

I checked the time on my phone. It was a few minutes after ten o'clock now. "I'm almost to Meira's to pick up some supplies." It would take me a good thirty-minute drive from Meira's house. If there was one thing I'd learned, it was that Meira didn't like to be rushed. If I tried, she'd most likely dig in her heels and make me wait longer. I figured my best approach was to concede at least half an hour to answering the questions she'd likely have ready for me. "I should be able to get there shortly after they do."

"Good." I could hear the relief in his voice.

We hung up, and I pulled back onto the road, driving the rest of the way to Meira's. She was sitting on her porch when I arrived, a cup of tea in her hand and a pensive look on her face.

"Tea?"

I knew better than to decline. "Please." By now, we had our routines. She'd offer me a cup of tea I didn't want, and I'd drink enough to appease her before launching into the real reason I was there. I thought of it as the price of admission.

I accepted the cup she poured from the tea set on the small table next to her. We drank in companionable silence for a minute.

"Some things are better left alone. Are you sure you need to do this?" Meira asked.

I took a deep breath. Grave robbing was not something I wanted to do, but I was willing to do it if it meant getting ammunition that could help against Masterson. "I do."

She held out a drawstring bag that had rested by her feet. "There's a ritual candle in here, along with instructions to perform the summoning. There are some other items you'll need to pick up."

I took the bag from her. I had expected her to insist on coming along. Her willingness to wash her hands of it told me just how distasteful she found the proposition of digging up an innocent's grave.

I fumbled the bag, the candle inside making a thud as it hit the porch floor. "The innocent child and the sacrifice," I mumbled, picking it back up.

Meira's eyes locked on mine. "What did you say?"

My heart sped up, and I broke out in a cold sweat. "Everyone assumed they were one and the same. The innocent child and the sacrifice." I turned to face her, working it out as I talked. "But what if they weren't?" I jumped to my feet. "You said it yourself. Masterson was a twin."

Meira went quiet as she considered it. "What are you saying?"

"I'm saying that the prophecy isn't about Claire and me—at least not entirely." I pulled out the sheet of paper I carried with me everywhere these days.

Meira stilled in her rocking chair, giving me her undivided attention as I read the key lines from the prophecy. "When they come, it will be as the innocent child and the sacrifice, as the corrupter and the destroyer."

Although I'd read those words hundreds of times, it wasn't until this reading that I considered an alternate possibility. "Claire is obviously the sacrifice, but what if the innocent child refers to Masterson's sister instead of Claire?"

Meira didn't react. Instead, she waited expectantly as I puzzled it out.

"Shit, how could I miss this?" I chastised myself. "Beleth is the king of temptation demons—the corrupter. And just like

I'm bound to Raum, Masterson is bound to Beleth." *Two souls bound through magic and bathed in blood.* And that was the key I'd missed. Demons didn't have souls. Only humans did. "Masterson and I are those two souls. He's the corrupter the prophecy refers to. And I am—"

"The destroyer," she finished, her eyes turning black.

I'd missed so many things that had been right in front of me. The demon inside her was but one of them.

I stared at the woman who had trained me. She was the picture of tranquility as she rocked gently, sipping her tea.

But all of it was a lie.

I revisited everything she taught me, every move she'd made, trying to pinpoint where the woman my grandmother had trusted had ceased to exist and this demon had taken her place. "You're the reason he's always one step ahead of us," I accused.

Her satisfied smile was that of the demon. "Yes."

I considered every time Masterson had gotten the jump on us. He'd beaten us to the shield because she knew where it was. She must have found out about the dagger Riley had stolen and tipped him off. I was sure she had told him about our trip to see Naomi, sealing her death warrant in the process.

Had she told him where to find Xavier, the fire elemental Masterson had turned into one of his hybrids? I'd suspected that a woman had been the one to attack him in Volkov's house, but I would have never suspected Meira. Now that I knew how easy a distortion spell was to use, it wasn't a stretch to imagine someone as powerful as a Tribunal member having a witch on standby to concoct one to hide a bruise.

How far back does her deception go? "How long have you been feeding Masterson information about us?"

"A long time, child." Meira set her teacup next to mine on the tray. When she turned to me, her face was schooled into its usual placid expression. "But then, deep down, I think you knew, didn't you? Always so suspicious." She clicked her tongue and looked down her nose at me. "It must really grate to discover those reservations you've been ignoring all this time were warranted."

I ran through every suspicion I'd had—every time I'd questioned her motives. It was true that Meira had helped me call Zepar when I was ready to send him back to hell, but short of helping me call him, she had aided him more than us. Once he was summoned, she'd turned on us quickly, attacking Riley on Zepar's command. *I missed so much.*

I thought again of every time Masterson seemed one step ahead of us. My head snapped up. "You are the one who told Masterson about Aldea." Like an idiot, I'd shown her the photos from Grandma Dottie's safe deposit box and told her that he was Claire's killer when I attacked Aldea at the Tribunal meeting.

She slow clapped, her face twisted into something ugly. "Beleth needed a way to ensure you accepted your demon. What better insurance than to dangle vengeance beneath your nose?"

My vision went hazy as Raum clambered to the surface. *She deserves to die for what she's done,* Raum insisted, struggling to break free of the stranglehold I had on him.

I clutched the arm of the chair to keep from launching myself at her. I needed answers more than I needed to vent my anger at her betrayal. "Why did you accept the demon, Meira?" Even though I knew the demon was in control of her, I still asked the question.

Meira tapped an elegant finger against her teacup. "We're not so different, you and I."

"What did he promise you in exchange for hosting a demon?"

Meira shrugged one elegant shoulder. "Does it matter?"

No. It doesn't matter. "You must have already had the demon in you when the Enclave sent the Shadow. That's why you ignored their instructions to teach me to hide my powers." My conversation with the Enclave representative was muddy, but I remembered her frustration that Meira hadn't followed directives.

Meira sneered. "I don't take orders from the Enclave's undead lackeys. Beleth had other plans for you. After those fools killed your sister, I needed to ensure you came into your full power."

Undead lackey. I frowned. "The Shadow wasn't Craig or Volkov?"

Meira laughed. "Of course not."

I thought back to those early days, and the vampire who had trailed after me like a bloodhound. Twitch had turned up around every corner, waiting in the shadows for a kill order that had never come. He had even delivered me to Meira's doorstep, yet I'd never suspected he was anything except the creepy stalker he appeared to be. The relief that Craig wasn't the Shadow was short-lived, shattering as the second half of her earlier statement hit me full in the chest.

After those fools killed your sister, she'd said.

I flashed back to the time I'd confronted her with the photo of her watching Claire play soccer. The man in the red baseball cap who had looked so familiar—why had I missed that? She'd been talking to Zepar when I'd come into her store. "You led them to Claire. Even then, you hosted the demon."

She waved a hand dismissively. "One of you had to die, anyway. The prophecy was quite clear about that."

I released my grip on the chair and stood in front of her, scanning her face for any trace of the woman my grandmother had called her friend. Then, I punched my palm into her chest and reached for the demon inside.

I'd once looked at Meira's soul and missed the demon bonded to it. Now that I held it, I knew why. Raum's bond was like a spliced wire, the crimson end of my soul fused to the black of the demon. Meira's demon was interwoven with the green of her soul. At first glance, the two were so entwined that they appeared like the dark green of the forest. But once I looked closer, I could separate the human soul and the demon into two strands.

It took me a long time to trace the soul through her body —to find the small nub of green still lodged in her chest. I worked on the bond even as her perfectly manicured hands clawed at my own, trying to pry them away as I unraveled the demon's hold. When I managed to separate them, I yanked the human soul to the surface and held it there. With my other hand, I ripped the demon from her body, watching it disintegrate before my eyes.

Meira gasped, her eyes opening wide as she took great gulping breaths like she'd just been drowning. After a minute, her breathing shallowed and her eyes focused on mine. She dropped her gaze to where my palm was splayed across her sternum. When she raised her eyes to mine again, they were filled with sorrow.

"I was there the whole time. I saw everything he did in my name." Meira swallowed.

I cupped her shoulder with my hand and gave it a squeeze. "It's not your fault."

She looked stricken at the thought of absolution. "I tried to fight him. At first, there were times when I could wrestle back control, but I was never strong enough to hold him off. He took over, and I was helpless to do anything about it."

I leaned in until we were eye to eye. "It's not your fault," I repeated. I kept my voice sure, even as the fear permeated me. Would this be my fate, as well? Sure, I was holding Raum at bay now, but how long would it be before he wore me down?

Meira must have seen the doubts clawing at me. She stiffened her spine. "We are not the same. You are stronger than I've ever been." She tapped my chest with a finger. "And he's weaker. He's not the same kind of demon I have, either."

From where I held the bond, I could sense the strength of the demon in Meira. And it was true that her demon felt more powerful than the one bonded to me. It was something that had nagged at me. Zepar, the first demon Beleth tried to marry me to, was infinitely more powerful than the one I ended up with. Until now, my working theory had been that he had given up on trying to summon stronger demons and settled for less powerful ones. But Meira had obviously been hosting a more powerful demon for a decade, which blew my theory out of the water.

"If Raum is a weaker demon, why did Beleth choose him instead of a stronger one?" I asked.

Meira glanced at my tattoo, guilt in her eyes.

"Beleth needed a divination demon to locate the demon artifacts."

Raum certainly checks that box.

Meira took a deep breath before unloading the rest. "Once Beleth has the artifacts, you'll be expendable. He only needed a demon strong enough to be a tool." She wouldn't meet my eyes even when she tried to put a more positive spin on it. "The good news is, with your strengths, Raum is a demon you can coexist with."

I wasn't so sure, but I held onto the hope she offered me with everything I had.

"I can do this." It was my mantra, now. If I said it enough, I prayed it would be true.

"You can," she said more forcefully. Her face softened as she looked at me. "You have your grandmother's eyes, you know."

Emotion clogged my throat, so all I could do was nod. Whenever I thought of my grandmother, there was always an ache at her loss. Lately, though, there was a rawness to my grief that hadn't been there since the early days after her death. I blinked until my vision cleared, and then I smiled. "So I hear."

"Your grandmother was the finest necromancer I ever knew. She pulled me out of a gutter and took me under her wing."

The thought of Meira in a gutter was too much for me to imagine. She'd always been the epitome of sophistication, from her silver locks to her cream and linen wardrobe. Everything about the woman screamed high class. The skepticism must have been plainly written across my face.

Meira smiled and leaned close. "It's true. I was a hellion in my early days." A look of nostalgia crossed her features. "A damn fine pickpocket, too."

It was too much for me to reconcile with the woman in front of me. Riley was going to have a field day with that information.

Meira's smile faded, and she looked off into the distance as she spoke. "Your grandmother taught me everything I knew. Dottie saw potential in me when everyone else looked at me with fear." Meira's voice broke as she spoke of my grandmother, and for a second, we were united in our love for her. When she spoke again, it was so faint I barely heard it. "And this is how I've repaid her."

I didn't have the words to assuage her guilt, but I stayed with her as she worked through it.

Because my hand was still planted against her chest, I felt the tremble as it racked her slight frame. "Masterson knows you plan to raise his sister tonight. He'll come for you."

Her confession didn't surprise me. As soon as I saw the demon within her, it was a foregone conclusion that our plan had been compromised.

"And we'll be ready for him when he does." I sounded far more confident than I felt, but it was worth the bluff to see the fear in Meira's eyes lessen. The demon she carried may have been responsible for so many tragedies that had befallen me, but the woman before me was as much Beleth's victim as I was. My grip on her soul was slipping, and I wanted her to go unburdened by the guilt I was intimately acquainted with. My grandmother would have wanted that.

Before I let go, though, I needed whatever intel I could glean. "Is there anything you can tell me about Beleth that can help us?"

Meira considered the question for a minute. "He's arrogant," she started. "And calculating. Beleth's only allegiance is to himself, and he wants to rule."

"Any weaknesses?" I probed, desperate for something that could give us an edge in this fight.

Meira swayed on her feet as her soul slipped a little more from my grasp. I held on tightly. "Masterson is both his strength and his weakness," she said finally.

"How so?"

"He needs Masterson to raise his army, and as long as Beleth needs him, he can't force Masterson to cede total control to him."

I frowned, trying to understand what she meant. The light in Meira's eyes was fading, and I knew I only had seconds left with her. "How is Masterson helping him raise an army?"

"The prophecy," Meira whispered.

Before I could question her further, I lost the tenuous hold I had on her soul. I watched it drift away, her body slumping into mine. I lowered her to the ground and wept.

After a few minutes, I rose to my feet and staggered inside her house. The inside of Meira's home was like a warm hug, all soft fabrics and shabby chic furnishings. I pulled the worn quilt throw from the back of her chair and carried it outside.

I closed Meira's eyes and covered her body with the quilt. I'd come back for her later, when this was all over, and we'd give her a burial worthy of a woman who had risen from a nobody in the streets to one of the most powerful necro-mancers in the world. For now, I picked up my phone and dialed Craig.

After I filled him in on what I'd learned, the line was quiet as he processed everything I'd just thrown at him. He'd known Meira even longer than I had, and though they hadn't been close, it was still hard to bear. Added to the loss was the galling fact that Beleth had managed to infiltrate our inner circle without any of us being the wiser for it.

"Are you there?" I asked after the silence stretched uncomfortably long.

"I'm here," he said. "I'll send someone for Meira."

I was grateful to let him handle it, not sure I could force myself to come back here once I left. "I'm leaving now. Are Riley and Volkov back yet?"

"Not yet," Craig said. "Why don't you head over to Volkov's. I'll let him know we're on our way there instead, and we can meet up there to hammer out the plan."

With the exception of Meira's farmhouse, Volkov's place was the most secluded of our homes. It also had the advantage of being a pack stronghold. Riley would argue that their security was subpar, but with shifters patrolling the grounds at Volkov's directive, it was the safest place we were going to find to regroup.

"I'll see you there."

CHAPTER 22

$\mathcal{B}$y the time we were all gathered in Volkov's living room, we had twelve hours left to prepare for our showdown with Masterson and his resident demon king. Craig had broken the news about Meira before I'd arrived.

Although I could tell Riley was bursting at the seams to give me the heist play-by-play, that was a story for the day after we faced Masterson. *If we live to tell it.* Instead, I shared my updated reading of the prophecy with everyone, including my theory that the prophecy was actually about both Masterson and me, along with our dead twin sisters.

As I talked, Volkov and Craig admired the infamous war scythe. I'd taken a quick look myself when we'd arrived, but I didn't seem to harbor the deep appreciation for bladed weapons that those two shared. Since Riley's interest in the war scythe ended the minute she successfully stole it, she had long since abandoned it, as well. She was now draped over one of Volkov's expensive living room chairs, her legs dangling over the side as we talked.

Riley let out a long-suffering sigh as she watched Craig

and Volkov handle the weapon like a long-lost lover. "If you two are finished fondling that scythe, can we get on with it?"

Volkov shot her an annoyed look, but he leaned the scythe against the wall and took a seat. Craig remained standing.

"What's the plan?" Riley asked the room at large.

I laid out what we knew. "Well, we know Masterson is going to show up at the cemetery tonight to interrupt my attempt at raising his dead sister. Meira told him when and where, so we can expect him to show up by midnight."

"We'll have to get everything in place before he gets there," Volkov said.

"Do you think he'll have eyes on the cemetery?" Craig asked.

I considered it. If it were any of us, we would definitely have someone camped out there watching for us. But both Masterson and Beleth were arrogant, and they had no reason to suspect Meira had tipped us off. I felt a tinge of sadness when I thought about her, but now that she was gone, so was our leak. "I don't think so, but we should have someone sweep the area just in case."

"I'll take care of it." Volkov slid his cell phone out of his pocket and tapped out a message. When he finished, he looked up. "I have a couple shifters on their way to the cemetery now. They'll do a sweep and then set up a perimeter watch."

"Great," I said. "So, we know where and when Masterson will show up. What kind of fire power do you think he'll bring?"

Craig stared at the weapon now leaning against the wall. "We can assume he's turned the missing fire elemental from Nevada, and we know he has at least one alpha shifter."

"I think it's a safe bet that he's turned several shifters,

given the missing person reports that have been trickling in," Volkov added.

Craig nodded. "Agreed. If I were Masterson, I'd also have a witch or two in my back pocket."

"Alright, so we assume he's coming with a contingent of soldiers," I summed up.

"And weapons?" Riley glanced at the war scythe. "We won that one, but he's got two to our one." She grimaced. "He's got the dagger and the shield."

I frowned. "And the shield is capable of deflecting any blows from the one weapon we do have."

I bit the inside of my cheek as I faced the facts. I was a far stronger fighter than I'd been a year ago. Between Krav Maga classes and training at the Compound, I could hold my own in a bar fight. Now that I could tap into Raum's powers, it gave me additional weapons in my arsenal. Thanks to Sato's instruction, I was even competent with a war scythe. Unfortunately, competent wasn't good enough, and everyone in this room knew it, even if no one wanted to say it out loud.

I caught Craig watching me, his face stoic as usual. From the slight pinch in his brow, I was telegraphing my worries. I ripped the Band-Aid off. "Let's face it. I'm no match for Masterson. With Beleth, he's powered by arguably the strongest demon alive—a demon with centuries of combat experience with the exact weapons he'll be fighting with." I dropped my head into my hands as the long odds we faced hit me. When I looked up again, all three of their faces were tight with worry. Even Riley lacked her usual bravado. "Armed with that dagger, he can kill me. All he needs to do is get close enough to strike."

Craig's expression darkened, and he gritted his teeth. "He won't get close enough." He crossed the room and crouched in front of me, tilting my chin so I'd look at him. "I will be your shield." He leaned closer and dropped his voice, so it was just for me. "And you will be my heart." His gray eyes were soft as he looked into mine, and there was a formality to his words that felt significant.

Something tugged in my chest as I reached for him, and I wondered if the mate bond had already taken root. If, by some miracle, we walked away from this, I was going to guard the love he offered as fiercely as he guarded me. I pulled Craig onto the couch next to me, and he gathered me against his side as if already in protector mode.

Volkov's pacing interrupted our moment. He stepped closer to us and tapped Craig on the arm. "You'll be the shield," he repeated, looking back at the scythe. "The dagger can cut through flesh and kill demons, but there's not a dagger forged that can penetrate stone. If you can keep her safe long enough that she can strike, we have a chance." Although Volkov's words were optimistic, he frowned as he tried to work out a winning strategy.

"I'm not going to win a demon fight," I said softly. Craig's grip tightened on my arm, lending me strength. I felt the pulse of power from Raum, and he, too, bled strength through our bond. But it wouldn't be enough. In a head-to-head match, Beleth would always be the stronger demon.

My head snapped up, and I stared at Riley. "What are you good at?"

"Stealing shit and getting out of binds," she answered without hesitation.

"And you?" I asked Volkov. "What are your strengths?"

"I'm an alpha," he said, stating the obvious.

I motioned for him to expand.

"As an alpha, I'm a powerful fighter in both human and

wolf form, my senses are superior, and I can compel other shifters with my alpha voice," he elaborated, not a hint of humbleness marring his self-assurance in his strengths.

"Most shifters," Riley corrected, lacing her hands behind her head and leaning back against her chair.

"Most shifters," he conceded.

I turned to face Craig. "As a gargoyle, you are virtually indestructible. You're an incredible fighter, and you can freaking fly."

He basked in my praise. "I have other skills, as well," he deadpanned.

"Gross!" Riley tossed a throw pillow at his head.

Craig caught it with a smirk and tucked it behind my head.

Volkov was leaning in now, interested in where I was going with all this. "What are you proposing?" he asked.

"I say we stop playing to his strengths and start playing to our own." After catching Riley's attention, I tossed her my phone. "First, we call in our friends. Then, we formulate a plan that draws on our collective strengths in order to kick some demon ass."

Riley jumped out of her chair, so she could high five me. "Hell yeah!" She looked down at my phone and then back at me. "The witches?"

I nodded. Although we should probably call Celeste, after Meira's betrayal, I didn't want to take chances on anyone I wasn't one hundred percent sure was in our corner. "Tell Helen to come armed for bear."

Riley laughed and skipped out of the room to make her call while Craig and Volkov stared at me.

"And your strengths?" Volkov asked, scanning me from head to toe, his eyes catching on the cute ballerina flats I'd slipped into this morning.

Craig growled, but I tugged him back against me. "I'm a costume designer." When both of them turned to stare at me, I laughed. "If there's one thing I know, it's how to put on a good show."

Riley came back into the room in time for my announcement. "Yessss." She fist-bumped me. "The witches are on it."

I grabbed her arm and headed for the door. "We need to get supplies."

Riley sidestepped to stand in front of Volkov, holding her hand out expectantly. When he just looked at her outstretched hand with a raised brow, she wiggled her fingers. "I'm going to need a Tribunal credit card. Surely, you don't expect us to pay for this out of pocket."

Volkov stood with a sigh, but he handed her a black Amex card from his wallet.

She beamed at him. "Sweet!"

"Supplies," he reiterated.

Riley waved him off as we headed for the door.

I paused on the threshold, and when I looked back, both men were staring blankly after us. I turned to Volkov first. "We're going to need your fog machines."

"What?"

"Your fog machines." When he continued looking at me blankly, I elaborated. "From Howl. Can you get them to the cemetery along with a generator?"

"Yes," he answered hesitantly.

"Good. We could also use some projector equipment, a few extension cords, and—" I turned to Riley with a shit-eating grin. "We're gonna need a sound system and strobe lights." I gave Craig a quick hug. "While you two come up with your battle plans, we're going shopping."

I paused to snap a few pictures of the war scythe on my

way out the door. Then, I locked my elbow with Riley's, and we left the two men staring dumbly after us.

"Where to?" Riley asked brightly as she climbed into the passenger side of my lemon-yellow Volkswagen Beetle.

"First, I need to call in a favor. Then, we're hitting up Cabela's."

Riley scooted forward in her seat and practically vibrated with excitement. "Hunting supplies?"

"Hunting supplies."

I started the engine, but before pulling out, I searched my phone for my ex-boyfriend's contact info. Gavin answered instantly. "Kali?"

Any other time, I'd ease into my ask, but the stakes were too high to waste time on small talk. "Hey Gavin. I'm sorry to call in another favor, but I have a rush job I need some help with. Could I get the contact info for your blacksmith friend?" As a professional jouster, Gavin's friend group was pretty eclectic, including a blacksmith he had on speed dial.

"Of course," he practically purred. "I'll text it to you now."

The details popped up on my screen. "Got it."

"I was thinking," Gavin started, but I cut him off before he could ask me to a friendly dinner in hopes of us getting back together.

"I'm sorry, Gavin, but I have to run." Riley waggled her brows suggestively as I talked. I swatted in her direction. "I'll catch you later."

Fortunately, Gavin's friend picked up the phone on the third ring. After introductions, I dangled an obscene amount of money for him to forge me a duplicate war scythe. "I'm texting you pictures now." After he confirmed he had received them, I asked how soon he could have it ready.

"Twelve hours," the blacksmith said.

"Yeah, I'm gonna need it in four."

He stuttered on the other end of the line, so I doubled the fee I had offered. "It doesn't have to be functional," I told him. "It just has to pass for it visually." After a protracted pause, he finally agreed. "There's going to be a rush fee."

"That's fine. You take credit cards, right?" These days, everyone had a credit card reader, so I crossed my fingers that he would, too.

"I do."

"Great!" I checked my watch. "I'll swing by to pick it up and pay for it at four o'clock."

That gave us four hours to load up on supplies before we needed to grab the look-alike scythe and head to the cemetery for setup. For the first time in weeks, I was in my element. By the time we were done, Beleth wouldn't know what had hit him.

Riley and I exchanged a smile before we buckled ourselves in for what was guaranteed to be a wild ride.

CHAPTER 23

When we arrived at the cemetery, the guys were already waiting for us. Volkov was barking orders to a small group of shifters gathered at the edge of the cemetery, while Craig scouted the area for the best spots to ambush our quarry.

"You can't park that here." Volkov looked affronted at the very existence of my cheery yellow car. "It's too distinctive."

I rolled my eyes. "I'm not parking here. I just need to unload, then I'll move the car."

Riley climbed out the passenger side and dug supplies out. She turned and handed a couple shopping bags to Volkov before going back for more.

He peered inside. Craig jogged up and looked over Volkov's shoulder, frowning at the bag full of camouflaged stocking caps and sweatshirts. Volkov fished around in the bag until he came up with a can of scent-blocking spray.

He wrinkled his nose. "Really?"

The last time I'd doused myself with deer piss, it hadn't worked. Werewolves' sense of smell was far too good for that.

I snatched the can back and smiled at him sweetly. "We're going to need all the distractions we can get." I pointed to the box strapped to the top of my car. "Can you have someone set this up over there?" I gestured to an area backed by trees.

Craig walked closer to the box, frowning as he read it. "A deer blind?"

"It's like a theme party," Riley chirped, handing Volkov his black Amex card.

Volkov pointed at the box on top of my car, his expression thunderous. "How the fuck much did that cost?"

I cringed. "Twelve hundred."

"Twelve hundred dollars?" He growled.

Riley crossed her arms. "Helen has bad knees."

Volkov stared at her. "What?"

She pointed to her legs. "You know, mobility issues?"

I thought of all the times I'd watched Helen climb shelves to reach something in her fabric store or march around to bark orders at everyone in her vicinity. Helen's knees seemed as good as mine, but I didn't contradict Riley.

Volkov stepped closer to Riley, his body crowding hers back against the car. "What the hell does that have to do with blowing over a grand of my money on a deer blind?"

Riley pulled a pack of gum out of her pocket and shoved two pieces in her mouth, then held the pack out to offer me one. I shook my head, not wanting to antagonize Volkov further.

Riley blew a giant bubble and popped it an inch from Volkov's face, forcing him to take a step back. "The eight-hundred-dollar one had shitty steps." She pointed to the card-board box holding the more expensive deer blind. "This one has nice, sturdy steps, and room for all three witches."

Craig bent his head closer to mine. "Why do the witches need to be in a deer blind?"

I grinned. "You'll see."

Volkov ran a hand through his dark hair and gradually unclenched his jaw. "You better have receipts," he grumbled.

Riley dug into her pocket and handed him the wad of receipts she'd stuffed there. Ignoring his grimace, she opened the car door and rummaged around until she found what she was looking for. After our stop at Cabela's, we'd hit up a clothing store on our way to the blacksmith. Cabela's might have had a clothing aisle, but even the threat of a demon war wouldn't get me to step foot in it. Riley handed Volkov the receipt from the bag before pulling out a black turtleneck and black yoga pants to toss at me.

I turned over the pants and checked the label before snorting and throwing them back to her. "Try again. These are too long."

Riley was a good three inches taller than me, and she had the long legs of a runner. She tossed me matching yoga pants that were shorter. Then she whipped her shirt over her head and shimmied into the turtleneck. Volkov growled at the group of shifters nearby until they looked at the ground. Riley winked at him before stepping out of her ripped blue jeans and yanking the yoga pants up around her waist.

I ducked into the back of the car to change my clothes. When I emerged, we looked like we were back in our teenage match-your-BFF phase. She grinned at me and pulled her bright pink hair back into a short ponytail to match mine. By the time we were done, every man in the vicinity was staring at us in confusion.

I winked at Craig. "Trust me. It's for a good cause."

Before I could explain further, Riley's witches arrived. I

quickly unloaded the rest of our supplies and recruited one of Volkov's shifters to park my car a few blocks away.

Alyce was the first to reach me, pulling me in for a grandmotherly hug. With her tightly curled slate-gray hair and portly figure, Alyce looked like the epitome of a sweet old lady even when she left the apron at home. Janis and Helen joined our huddle, while Bea checked out the hot shifters milling around.

Helen put a hand on her hip, emphasizing her thin frame. "Okay, girls. Where do you need us?"

Riley had called them and put them on speaker phone as we ran our errands. We'd already hashed out the basics in the car, so that just left logistics.

I turned to Janis, who was in charge of spell casting. "Let's save the makeover for closer to midnight." Janis nodded. "Follow me, and I'll show you where we'll need the barrier spell." Janis trotted after me as Riley shoved camouflage at the remaining ladies and shooed them into the trees to get changed.

The cemetery was located just outside the city on a picturesque hillside. On three sides, the cemetery was bordered by trees. The remaining side was the one I was concerned about because across the street was dotted with houses. Although they were a fair distance away, the residential area was well within hearing distance. Plus, once night fell, the ruckus we were going to create would definitely draw attention.

After explaining what I wanted, I looked at Janis. She paced along the roadway, laying small stones at four- or five-foot intervals.

"Can you do it?" I asked her.

She straightened and smiled at me. "Easy peasy."

I left her to it and rejoined the others.

By now, the old witches had drawn a crowd. I waved to get Craig's attention and motioned for him and Volkov to join us.

"All set?" I asked them. The two of them had been busy getting their fighters up to speed.

"Everyone's in position," Volkov said.

"And earbuds?" Riley asked as she joined us.

Volkov nodded. Because we didn't want to risk Masterson compelling those on our side to do anything, all Volkov's men were wearing noise-canceling earbuds that would block out all sound except for the radio frequency they were tuned to for communicating with the team. Rather than carting around bulky walkie-talkies like it was the nineteen eighties, we had all downloaded an app on our cell phones so we could coordinate during the fight. Riley passed out the remaining earbuds to the witches, saving a set for each of us. I was pretty sure I couldn't be compelled, but we'd decided not to take any chances.

Once everyone was huddled around, I ran through the plan.

"We're going to set up in zones. Our goals are to disorient, disrupt, and disguise." I pointed to a small grove of trees at the edge of the cemetery where the shifters were still setting up the deer blind. Because we'd splurged for the twelve-hundred-dollar model, it was both solid and roomy. When fully assembled, the deer blind would be like a tent on stilts, giving the witches a clear vantage point while keeping them away from the worst of the fighting. The flaps on all sides of the blind could be rolled up, which would accommodate shooting in all directions.

"Helen, Alyce, and Bea, you'll be in there. Did you bring your guns?"

Helen cackled and dug around in the duffle bag she'd carried with her. She pulled out her trusty paintball gun and several brown paper bags full of her special stash of paintballs, leaving the remaining two guns at the bottom of the duffle.

Riley leaned in to get a closer look. "What'd you bring?"

Helen brandished the bags in the air. "I've got stink bombs."

"Classic," Riley murmured.

Helen reached inside and pulled out a mud-colored ball. "And stun bombs. These hurt like a sonofabitch if they hit you. Like a thousand bee stings." She reached out and pinched Alyce on the arm to demonstrate her point.

"Ouch!" Alyce jumped but then reached for one of the stun bombs to tuck into the oversized pocket of her camouflaged sweatshirt.

"And these," Helen announced, pulling out a handful of sparkly pink numbers, "are flash bombs. They'll temporarily blind anyone looking straight at them."

Craig groaned. "What if you ladies accidentally blind us instead of the enemy?"

Helen turned to him, outrage stamped all over her face. "Are you saying I'm a crap shot?" she challenged.

Craig held up his hands in defeat. "I'm just saying maybe we need a code word for a warning."

Alyce nodded solemnly. "That's a good idea." She examined the sparkly balls. "How about we yell 'jizz?'"

Craig smothered his laugh, while Volkov choked and coughed into his fist. Alyce smiled sweetly at them both.

"Good thinking," Bea agreed, slapping Volkov on the back. "You okay there, sugar?"

Before things had a chance to go further downhill, I laid out the rest of the plan Riley and I had concocted. There would be three zones. Zone one would be the open clearing outside the fenced-in cemetery that faced the houses across the street. Zone two consisted of the cemetery proper. And zone three was the perimeter tree line surrounding the cemetery on three sides.

Janis would be in zone one maintaining the barrier spell. It would prevent anyone from seeing or hearing what went on beyond zone one. Several shifters would be stationed in zone one to protect Janis and funnel Masterson's group where we wanted them. They'd also communicate numbers and types of soldiers that Masterson brought with him, allowing us to adjust our plan of attack as needed.

Volkov's men had set up the fog machines in zone two. Once the scouts spotted Masterson and crew, we'd fire them up. They'd provide cover for the fighters located throughout the cemetery. We had also bought a cheap sprayer and enough scent-blocking spray to blanket the entire cemetery with it. Although it would be an irritant for all of the shifters in the vicinity, ours were expecting it. I was hoping it would screw with the senses of Masterson's shifters enough that they would have difficulty distinguishing individual scents. That would offer our fighters some additional cover as well as prevent the shifters from telling Riley and me apart.

Riley and I would be at the far end of the cemetery with Volkov and Craig. Riley would give me the cover I needed to land a lucky shot. And Craig and Volkov would be on protection duty, increasing the odds that Riley and I would walk out of this cemetery alive.

I'd made Riley swear that as soon as she felt in imminent danger, she'd drop the spell and run. Although she'd agreed, I wasn't sure I trusted she'd follow through in time to escape. I wasn't above knocking her out if that's what it took to keep her alive, so I planned to keep a close eye on her during the fighting.

The witches would camp out in zone three. Their role was shock and awe. Between them shooting spelled paint bombs and the sound system and strobe lights rigged up in the trees, it should keep Masterson's crew off-kilter enough for us to attack.

I checked my watch. "Two hours until showtime. Does everyone know what they're supposed to do?"

Two dozen heads nodded in unison. I teared up as I looked around at their faces. Some of them I'd come to love. Others I barely knew. But all of them had turned up when I needed them, willing to put themselves on the line for me. Craig came up behind me, wrapping his arms around my waist. I leaned my head against his chest and took a steadying breath.

"If things go sideways, you do what you need to do to save yourself," I told the crowd. There were some grunts of argument, but no one spoke up. I had to say it, even if none of them listened. I spotted Riley among them, her bright-blue eyes locking with mine.

She raised her fist in the air. "Let's kick us some demon ass!"

A collective roar went up, and I was thankful Janis had the foresight to erect the barrier spell early.

Riley made her way to me, Volkov close behind her. She leaned in for a quick hug. "We've got this." Riley reached for the replica war scythe that matched my own. "Now, let's go find Janis for our makeovers."

The only thing freakier than standing face-to-face with my doppelgänger was looking in a mirror and seeing Riley's face gazing out at me. I touched the tips of my now bright-pink locks and widened my startling blue eyes at what I saw. After scrunching up my nose and stretching my mouth into various contortions, I handed the mirror to Riley.

She turned her head from side to side, admiring Janis's handiwork. "How long will the spell last?"

Janis accepted the mirror Riley handed over. "About two hours."

I checked the time. We still had about an hour until show-time. My battle experience was limited to movies and board games, so I had no idea how long a typical battle took. *An hour is probably fine.*

I handed Riley back the faux war scythe I'd been holding while she'd looked in the mirror. Gavin's blacksmith had done a bang-up job with the replica. At first glance, it was indistinguishable from the real one. The only thing saving us from mixing them up was the camo tape I'd wrapped around mine to mark the correct hand positions. While Cabela's sold everything from hunting gear to fudge, they apparently didn't keep cute baby chick washi tape in stock, so camouflage duct tape it was.

Riley and I headed toward the older section of the cemetery where Masterson's sister was buried. Craig and Volkov had their heads bent together discussing last-minute strategy as we approached. When they caught sight of us, they stopped abruptly and stared.

Riley nudged me with her hip and bent to my ear. "Do you think they can tell the difference?"

Craig's eyes locked on mine and his lips quirked up.

"Oh yeah." I stopped in front of him and waited for his reaction.

He tugged on my pink ponytail. "Nice hair."

"Thanks," Riley beamed. She checked the area around the grave to make sure everything was set up for the ritual.

Because there was no need to actually dig up Masterson's sister to perform a fake ritual, we'd opted for piling fresh dirt on top of the gravesite instead. At a glance, it would look as if the grave had been disturbed. Riley lit the candles perched on top of the tombstone. Next to them lay a collection of objects I hoped would pass for a typical necromancer ritual setup. Since Meira had never gotten to the part about how other necromancers raised the dead, we were improvising. An ornate chalice sat on the tombstone between the candles. I remembered Meira mentioning something about herbs, but a quick Google search proved more confusing than enlightening. We'd settled for dumping an old bag of potpourri on top of the tombstone. On the plus side, it made the area around the grave smell nice.

Riley stuck her war scythe in the handy-dandy fishing pole

holder she'd insisted on adding to our Cabela's haul. Even though the guys had looked appalled at her ingenuity, I'd thought it was a stroke of genius. She'd found one that came with a spike, which she'd driven into the ground next to the grave. The handle of the war scythe fit snugly inside. Because it held the scythe at an angle, it was grab and go. *Brilliant.*

I gave Riley a thumbs up, and she grinned at me. "All set."

Craig and I moved several tombstones over to where we'd wait for our opening to attack Masterson.

Volkov held his hand up to his ear, listening intently. He flicked his finger in the air to indicate we should all turn on our communication apps. I quickly toggled the volume higher on my ear buds.

"We've got eyes on Masterson. He's two blocks out and closing in on foot." There was a slight pause before the shifter came back on air. "We're counting half a dozen hybrids, including a fire elemental. Two of them are stuck to Masterson's side. Take them out first if you can."

Craig and I looked at each other, and his shoulders relaxed a little. *Good. That's what we've been expecting.* I surveyed the cemetery, watching as everyone moved into position. With several of Volkov's shifters in the mix, we outnumbered them almost two to one. Just as I began breathing a little easier, our scout's voice cut in.

"Shit. They're not alone. He's got a dozen vampires fanning out. They'll be coming at the cemetery from all directions."

Volkov swore. He grabbed Riley by the arm and spun her to face him. "Remember, you're there to create a distraction. That's all. Do not engage Masterson. And for fuck's sake, don't antagonize him. Stick to the plan."

"Yeah, yeah." Riley shook off his hands. "One fake sacrificial goat coming right up." She cracked her neck as she moved into position.

Without another word, Volkov shucked off his clothes and transformed into his wolf. I stumbled back a step. This was the first time I'd seen him change. The only other werewolf I'd seen change had been Ruby almost a year ago. Unlike Ruby's transformation, Volkov's was almost instantaneous, with none of the awkward contortions or grunts of pain. One second, he was a man, and the next, a huge wolf stood in his place. Volkov in human form was scary enough. As a wolf, he was terrifying. He was easily twice the size of a normal wolf, with a jet-black coat and wicked glowing amber eyes.

Barely leashed violence was written in every line of his body. When Volkov bared his teeth, I stumbled back into Craig.

Craig bent his head to my ear. "I've got your back."

We will kill the false king and feast on the eyes we pluck from his skull, Raum added helpfully.

Dude. Gross. We're not doing that.

I shoved my fear aside and forced myself to focus on what needed to be done. I felt the change in the air as Craig shifted behind me, his presence at my back a reassuring wall of stone and strength.

Riley pulled a ketchup packet out of her pocket and palmed it. Then, she lifted an ornamental dagger in the air with her right hand and waited for Masterson to appear. Volkov stood off to her side, hackles raised. Nervous energy filled me as the minutes drew out, agonizingly long.

When the shifters in zone one fired the machines up, a dense fog blanketed the ground and rolled through the cemetery. The mobile projectors were on, casting the shadowy shapes of werewolves into the trees. My heart raced as the fighting began. Craig gripped my shoulder, and I adjusted my grip on the war scythe. I held it blade-side down, so anyone looking my way would think I held a common bo staff instead of the weapon capable of killing a demon.

"Ready?" Craig's voice in gargoyle form rumbled like gravel.

I dropped into a fighter's stance and drew power through my bond with Raum. "Ready."

And then all hell broke loose.

When Masterson stepped through the rolling fog, he was flanked by a fire elemental with hands like flamethrowers and a giant hybrid with the eyes of a vampire and the build of a gorilla shifter. Between them, Masterson appeared harmless. Whereas everyone around him looked like the killers they were, Masterson looked like a computer programmer who had wandered into the fray. But I knew better. Beneath that unassuming exterior was the most powerful demon to walk the earth.

Behind them, Masterson's vampires fought fang and claw with Volkov's shifters. The vampires moved so fast they were hard to track with the human eye. If it weren't for the shifters' heightened senses, it would have been a massacre. As it was, the two sides tore into each other like rabid beasts, blood staining the ground where they fought.

Masterson immediately zeroed in on Riley. With a sharp command, the fire elemental at his side let loose a stream of fire at a group of shifters who were moving in from the side. Janis was ready for him, though, and the fire flickered over the shield she'd erected. I breathed a sigh of relief when the shield held steady.

As the group fought its way closer to the center of the cemetery where Riley was, Helen and company let loose with the spelled paintballs. Thanks to my earbuds, I could hear the witches cackling as one hit the fire elemental dead center in the chest. Based on his sudden gagging, it was probably a stink bomb, but he recovered quickly and threw another ball of fire toward the deer blind the witches were using for cover. Fortunately, it fell well short of the target.

"Incoming jizz," Bea shouted gleefully. "Cover your eyes!" Although several shifters laughed despite the very real threats all around them, they got their hands up in time to shield their eyes from the flash bombs that sailed through the air.

Masterson's crew wasn't so fortunate. They stuttered to a halt, blinking to clear their eyesight. The witches doubled down, pelting them with another round of flash bombs, followed by stun bombs. The fire elemental swatted at his body as the stun bomb did its job, allowing one of Volkov's shifters to slide in behind him. Claws extended, the shifter sliced cleanly through his jugular. When the elemental stopped struggling, the shifter tossed his body over his shoulder and ran toward us.

Another round of flash bombs gave me the opening I needed. I concentrated on the spiritual plane, scanning the fire elemental's body for the demon residing within. As soon as I saw it coiled like a snake in his chest, I grabbed ahold of it and yanked, severing the bond with a quick snap of my wrist. I signaled to the shifter that it was done, and he dumped the elemental's body on the ground to rejoin the fight. With the fire elemental out of commission, I liked our odds a whole lot better.

Riley sliced into the ketchup packet, letting it ooze through her fingers like blood. For making it up on the fly, she was putting on a pretty convincing performance. Then, she began chanting. She hadn't bothered to mute herself, so her improv blasted over everyone's earbuds. Riley drew on all those nights at karaoke as she belted out the lyrics to Eminem's "Lose Yourself."

"Your mic is on, Riley," Volkov grumbled, cutting her off.

There was a beat of awkward silence, and then a full-throated chorus before Riley finally muted herself. I bit back a smile but sobered when I spotted Masterson fighting his way closer to her.

I prepared to launch as soon as I saw an opening. I'd only get one chance, so I needed to be sure to time it right. That meant letting him get to Riley and trusting Volkov would keep her safe until I could get close enough to strike. A quick glance at Craig behind me told me the waiting was just as difficult for him as it was for me. He was used to leading the charge, not hanging back like this. But he did it for me.

When one of the shifters got the drop on Masterson's hybrid who was flanking him on the right, I felt a surge of hope. They'd done it. By taking out his bodyguards, the shifters had cleared a path for my attack. Even with the demon artifact dagger clutched in his hand, Masterson was vulnerable. A six-inch dagger was no match for the reach of my war scythe. *This crazy-ass plan is going to work.* Adrenaline surged through me at the taste of victory.

Nothing was ever that simple, though.

Thanks to the noise-canceling earbuds, I didn't hear the hand clawing its way up through the grave, so the bony grasp on my ankle made me leap a foot in the air and shriek like a little girl.

"What the hell?" I shouted, kicking my foot until I broke free.

Craig lifted me off my feet and backpedaled away from the dead body crawling its way out of the earth. I scanned the cemetery and saw others all around us. Back here, the graves were old, the bodies decayed. When they emerged from their graves, they were little more than bones. Toward the front of the cemetery were the fresh graves, and those bodies were more horrifying as they broke the ground. *How is this possible?*

I turned my sights on Masterson, watching his lips move. Since I was fairly confident that Masterson wouldn't be able to compel me, I yanked the earbuds from my ears before Craig could stop me. I needed all my senses online for what came next. I was too far away to make out Masterson's words, but there was no question that Masterson was the one doing this. When I saw his eyes, the last puzzle piece clicked into place. Even from this distance, I could see that his eyes were light instead of the pitch black of the demon as I'd been expecting.

Before she'd died, Meira had claimed Masterson was helping Beleth raise his army. I'd assumed she'd meant an army of hybrids. I'd never considered she meant an army of the dead, even when she'd pointed me to the prophecy. The prophecy that warned of dangers—plural—born into this world. Meira had once told me I was more powerful than other necromancers because I had been born a twin. When my sister died, I'd absorbed her power, and that amplified my own. I'd assumed the power referred to in the prophecy had been me, and that ego-centric reading crowded out the truth.

Masterson was also a twin, one whose sister was born a necromancer. None of us had considered that he could be one, too, because necromancers had always been female. The prophecy rang in my head, so obvious now that I couldn't believe I'd missed it before:

twins birthed on the eve of a new moon
with power unlike the world has seen

for they shall be able to call forth demons
and command whole armies of the dead.

All around me, proof of his power dragged themselves from graves. Despite the shifters still fighting, they were now vastly outnumbered by the dead under Masterson's control.

"We have to help them," I yelled, darting forward.

Craig's hand landed on my arm, and for a second, I thought he'd stop me. Instead, he beat his wings and lifted us into the air, wrapping an arm around my waist. He landed behind the shifters, and we fought side by side against the dead.

Like vampires, decapitation seemed to stop them. I swung my scythe in wide arcs, taking as many out as I could. Craig was more hands-on, ripping their heads from their bodies. But there were only two of us, and a hundred of them. We were losing ground by the minute. Panic rode me as I watched the dead surround Riley and Volkov, tightening the circle like a noose.

Masterson was closing in on Riley fast. She grabbed her war scythe and brandished it like it was real. I needed a weapon that could cut through the masses, and I wished for the twentieth time that Liv was here to fight on our side. I needed fire, and since we didn't have Liv, there was only one other way to get it. I searched for the discarded body of the fire elemental, finding it close to where Riley and Volkov now fought off their attackers. Masterson stood back, watching and waiting for Riley to weaken. *Fuck that.*

To reanimate the elemental, I needed a soul. When I snapped my vision to the spiritual plane, there were several newly departed souls nearby to choose from, but despite my rising desperation, forcing those lost souls into the body felt wrong. Instead, I called to an older soul I already had a bond with.

Jack Gates appeared in the middle of the battle, his close-cropped red beard making him easy to spot. Whether it was due to his profession as a seasoned reporter or the time he'd spent tagging along with me in the supernatural world, Jack didn't panic. He searched the battle until his eyes found mine staring at him.

"I need your help," I shouted over the din of fighting. I pointed to the body of the fire elemental.

Jack looked toward Riley and Volkov, who were still fighting Masterson's dead soldiers, then looked back at me. He squinted as he studied me. He spoke too quietly for me to hear from this distance, but I read the question on his lips. "You can see me?"

It took me a second to realize he thought he was talking to Riley. "Long story," I yelled, pointing at myself. "But it's me, Kali." I pointed back at the body. "Will you help?"

Jack huffed, but he dove inside the dead body. He stood on shaky legs, holding his hands out in front of himself. When they lit on fire, Jack screeched and waved them around in the air trying to put them out.

"You're fine!" I assured him. "Aim them at the fricking zombies." I wasn't sure they technically qualified as zombies since they weren't eating brains, but Jack caught on anyway. As fire shot from his hands and into the crowd of the dead, a path opened.

Because we didn't want to tip Masterson off, Craig and I kept to the ground as we moved in. We ran through the ring of burning bodies in time to see Masterson lunge for Riley. Volkov jumped in front of her, teeth bared and snarling. Masterson smiled at the wolf and held his dagger ready. Riley swung the faux war scythe haphazardly at Masterson's head, and it gave Volkov the opening he needed to dart forward and latch on to Masterson's thigh. Volkov fought as viciously as I had always suspected him capable of. With a quick jerk of his head, Volkov tore a chunk of flesh off the leg in his mouth.

Even with those jaws, he was no match for a demon as strong as Beleth. The dagger caught Volkov on his haunches. With a roar, Volkov leapt away, careful to keep himself between Riley and Beleth despite his injury.

When Masterson went for him again, I saw my opening. I gave Riley our agreed-upon signal. She shifted into her goat form as he lunged at her with the dagger. Masterson hit nothing but air, and Riley bleated at him right before she headbutted his leg. Volkov growled, grabbing her by the scruff of her neck. Riley went limp in his jaws like one of those fainting goats on YouTube. If we hadn't been in the fight for our lives, I would have laughed.

Instead, I stayed focused on my kill shot. I swung my scythe for Masterson's neck as he spun around to face me, eyes lighting with recognition despite the face I wore. My scythe struck bone, but the swing hadn't been strong enough to cut clean through.

I yanked on my weapon, but not fast enough. Masterson grabbed the handle and whipped his head to the side, bringing me with it. He had to drop the shield to attack with his other hand. His strike was lightning fast as he went for my heart.

Craig was faster. Craig wrapped a wing around me, and Masterson's dagger bounced off stone and clattered to the ground.

My scythe came free, and this time, I put the full power of the demon behind my swing. My racing heartbeat slowed, and my fear dissipated as Raum took over, relegating me to a spectator. This time, Masterson's head came off his shoulders and landed at my feet. Beleth left Masterson's body and burst into flames before disintegrating into nothing. All around us, the bodies of the dead collapsed, and the sounds of battle died out.

Although we'd won, I didn't celebrate. In order to kill Beleth, I'd pulled too much power, and Raum had taken over. It was like being trapped in the fog as I watched the aftermath through a demon's eyes. My soul battered against my rib cage like a bird with a broken wing, but no matter how hard I beat against my body, I couldn't rise up again.

It wasn't until I stilled, the fight leaving my body, that I saw the faint silver strand threaded through the oily black bond. I knew it instantly for what it was—the mate bond that had begun to form between Craig and me. Without hesitation, I latched onto it, and I followed that thin sliver thread until I found my way back to him. When I opened my eyes, Craig cradled my body in his arms, those stormy gray eyes blotting out the carnage all around us.

He leaned closer, resting his forehead against mine. "I've got you."

CHAPTER 25

"Absolutely fucking not," Volkov snarled. Although his right leg was still bandaged from Masterson's attack—a stab to the bone from a dagger forged in hellfire apparently healed slowly even for an alpha wolf—Volkov looked like he was ready to rip the head off of our visitor.

It would make a nice ball, Raum said happily.

Kage Sato leaned casually against the counter in my shop and smiled at Volkov. In his skinny jeans and Puff the Magic Dragon t-shirt, it would be easy to underestimate him. "You have no say in the matter," he said.

Volkov's body tensed in anticipation of a fight, but he made no move toward Sato. "You can't be serious about this." He gave me the once-over before shaking his head in disgust. "She has zero qualifications. She was a walking menace before she bonded with that demon. Now—"

"Choose your words carefully, my friend." Craig leveled Volkov with a stone-cold glare.

Now we are a force to be reckoned with. Raum and the Destroyer.

I snorted and everyone looked at me. I waved a hand in the air. "Carry on."

Volkov clenched and unclenched his jaw for several seconds before finishing. "She is too young and too inexperienced to take Meira's place on the Tribunal."

"The Enclave has chosen her to serve on the Tribunal. So, it shall be so." Sato's voice rang with finality.

I snapped my fingers in the air to get everyone's attention. "And if I don't want to be on some stuffy-ass Tribunal?"

When Volkov had called to let us know that an Enclave representative was on the way and that everyone's presence was required, I'd insisted we meet here—all six of us, if you counted Jack Gates, who dropped by unannounced a few minutes after Sato arrived. I was still emotionally raw from the fight with Masterson and reeling from Meira's deception. Whatever bombshell the Enclave was prepared to drop—and with them, it was always a bombshell—I had wanted it to be on my home turf, not Volkov's. So here we were.

Surrounded by racks of handmade costumes and plastic swords, the idea of getting roped into endless meetings and petty politics held no appeal.

Sato studied me. "They've authorized me to negotiate terms."

Riley propped her head on her hands. She was sitting cross-legged on the counter, elbows on her knees, watching the show. "This shit is rich. You should ask for a fat bank account and a lifetime supply of Xanax to deal with these fools."

"You're going to need my help if you want to get into politics," Jack said. "I have the experience to help you navigate and root out corruption."

I sighed and shooed Jack away.

He didn't budge. "Think it over. I could be a great asset." He waited until I nodded before disappearing to wherever he hung out when he wasn't harassing me. After his help with Masterson, I owed him big time, so I was trying to be more welcoming when he popped by.

"Hard pass," I said, watching for Sato's reaction.

Of course, Sato was the master of ignoring objections. He turned to Riley. "Speaking of fat bank accounts, the Enclave would like to offer you employment."

"What kind of employment?" Riley asked.

Injured or not, Volkov lunged for Sato, grabbing him by the shirt and lifting him off the ground. "Leave her out of this."

Sato smiled down at Volkov, then struck the center of his chest with his palm, sending the larger man careening into the counter. Sato landed on his feet like a cat.

"Whoa," Riley said. "I did not see that coming." She gave Sato an assessing look. "I'm listening."

"The Enclave is aware of your unique skillset, and they'd like to hire you to retrieve the remaining demon artifacts for them," Sato said.

"Hold up." Riley uncrossed her legs and jumped off the counter, crowding closer to Sato. "You're telling me they want to pay me to steal for them?"

"Yes. They'll pay you fifty-thousand dollars per artifact plus expenses." Sato waited for her answer.

"Absolutely not," Volkov argued. "It's too dangerous." He turned amber eyes on Riley. "We just lost ten seasoned fighters in the battle against Beleth. You're not going to be the next casualty."

"You're right. I'm not." Riley crossed her arms over her chest and considered Sato. "One hundred thousand plus expenses and no interference. You give me the job, then stay out of it. I do the jobs my way, with my people."

"Done."

Riley kicked the wall. "I should have asked for more."

Sato winked at her. "You really should have."

From the look of Volkov, his wolf was seconds from slipping his leash. He glared at Riley. "Don't do it."

Volkov and I were on the same page about this.

"Riley, think about what you'd be getting into," I urged. "With Beleth gone, it's going to be a demon free-for-all. The other kings will be hunting for those artifacts, trying to consolidate power."

"Not just the kings," Sato said. "Vampires will be searching for them, as well, trying to secure them for their kings. I won't lie to you. This will be more dangerous than any job you've done."

Riley tipped her chin up, and I knew she was going to take the job before she said a word. "Noted. I'm going to need an advance for expenses."

Sato nodded solemnly. "I'll be your handler."

Volkov growled and stalked closer until the two men were chest-to-chest.

Sato sighed. "That means I will be the go-between. I'll give you the assignments when we get word about an artifact, and I will retrieve the artifacts once you've secured them."

Volkov didn't back down. "You'll get her killed."

A flash of hurt crossed Riley's face, and I knew she was taking all of our concern as not believing she could do it. She was wrong. If anyone could steal those artifacts, it was her.

"I'll take the Tribunal position on two conditions," I said, breaking up the fight brewing.

Craig bent his head to mine. "Are you sure?"

I nodded.

"What are your conditions?" Sato asked, ignoring the alpha who was still looming over him.

"You're here to secure the weapons and take them back to the Enclave, correct?" I tapped Volkov on the shoulder and waited until he reluctantly stepped aside so I could meet Sato's eyes.

"I am."

"Condition one. Riley keeps the dagger."

Sato studied me for several seconds. "That dagger is dangerous in the wrong hands."

"Agreed," I said. "That's why it needs to be in the right hands. You're asking her to go up against vampires and demons to steal these artifacts for you. That dagger gives Riley a way to defend herself while she does it."

"Done."

Everyone breathed easier. Riley held her hand up for a high five but thought better of it and pulled me in for a hug. Even Volkov's battle-ready posturing relaxed slightly, a resigned expression on his face as he watched Riley and me.

"And condition two?" Sato asked.

I sighed. "I want the Chihuahua."

Sato laughed. "You want Aleksei's dog?"

Volkov looked between us like we'd both lost our minds. Admittedly, the idea of Aleksei with a pocket-sized dog would have been unbelievable had I not seen it for myself. But Raum and I had come to a tenuous agreement. He'd be my wingman, but he wanted the dog. I didn't totally trust him, of course. He was a demon, after all. But I kind of missed the little spitfire myself, and it would at least keep Raum appeased for a while.

"Alright." Sato was still chuckling. "I'll bring you your dog."

Raum vibrated with excitement. *We'll name him Raum the Almighty and bring him the finger bones of our enemies to gnaw on.*

Or, I suggested, *we could buy chew toys from the pet store.*

Before he left, Sato had both Riley and me sign binding agreements while Volkov paced in the background. Then, I turned over the shield and war scythe to Sato's capable hands. Since he had no idea I had smuggled the orb from the island, I didn't mention it.

Emma came in just as he was leaving. She eyed the weapons he carried as she held the door open for him. "Wow! Those are killer replicas. Did we get a new prop shipment in while I was out?" she asked.

She has no idea. Emma may have been one of my best friends, but she was human, which meant she was blissfully unaware of everything that had happened. As far as she knew, Volkov had stabbed himself in the thigh with an arrow. Riley had smirked when she'd come up with that one.

"One of a kind, I'm afraid." I pulled her in for a hug. "I've missed you, Em."

She laughed but squeezed me back. "We just saw each other."

I whistled to get everyone's attention. "I have a surprise."

Riley did her version of a happy dance, hip-bumping Emma and knocking her off balance. Volkov and Craig watched me warily, but I ignored them. We were all due for a little fun.

"Stay here." I went to the back of the shop and grabbed one of the boxes of costumes I'd brought back from Romania.

I set it on the counter and unfolded the flaps. "Emma scored us a booth at the Kansas City Renaissance Festival this year!" I could barely contain my excitement. "We're gonna be the hottest costume shop there. I thought we could all go together."

I pulled out Emma's costume first, handing her one of my top three creations ever—a gorgeous floor-length corseted dress made with layers of tulle attached to the skirt. The bodice of the dress had taken hours to craft, with glass beads and silk flowers cascading over the shoulder down to the waist.

Emma gasped when she saw it and immediately burst into tears. "It's the most beautiful thing I've ever seen. You made this for me?"

I nodded, crying because she was crying. I wiped my eyes with a laugh.

While Emma's costume had taken the longest—by far—to create, I'd put a lot of thought into everyone's costume. I reached for Riley's next, as she peered over my shoulder to get a look.

"Is that what I think it is?" she asked, a twinkle in her eye.

"Sure is." I shook out the velvet-lined red hooded cloak and draped it around her shoulders.

Volkov narrowed his eyes when I added the thrifted picnic basket to her outfit, and Craig grinned at me.

Riley skipped around the room before stopping in front of Volkov. "I love everything about this costume." She twirled and then tapped him on the nose.

I pulled out two of the men's costumes, leaving Bennie's in the box to give to him later.

Volkov scowled down at the costume I handed him. "This is for me?"

Riley squeezed his bicep and grinned from ear to ear. "This is going to be so much fun."

Both men blanched at her enthusiasm, but they took the medieval pants and cloaks.

"Thank you," Craig mumbled as he stared down at the form-fitting tights that had fueled more than one fantasy while I had been away. I'd made Volkov trousers because there were some things I wouldn't be able to unsee. Craig cleared his throat and held up the tights. "These are going to put on quite the show."

I bit my lip and wrinkled my nose. "That's the idea."

"Get out," he barked. Everyone laughed, but he hustled them all out the door and locked it behind them.

When he turned back to me, my knees almost buckled at the hunger in his eyes. He picked me up without breaking stride and carried me into the back room, shoving fabric and sewing supplies out of the way to sit me on the worktable.

"You know," I teased. "Now that I'm officially on the Tribunal, it kind of makes me your boss."

His smile was all gargoyle. "Then, I guess we'd better get started establishing a working relationship." Craig pulled me close, and our bond flared a little brighter.

Looking into his steely eyes, I relaxed for the first time in months. Whatever came for us, we'd face it together.

If you enjoyed this book, please consider leaving a review or rating on Amazon and/or GoodReads. Your reviews help new readers discover my books and are always appreciated!

If you'd like to be notified of new releases and exclusive content, you can sign up for my newsletter at lamcbride.com/ newsletter/ and join my Facebook Readers Group at https:// www.facebook.com/groups/lamcbridereaders

BOOKS BY L.A. MCBRIDE

KALI JAMES SERIES

Book 1: Fastening the Grave

Book 2: Threading the Bones

Book 3: Stitching the Talisman

Book 4: Gathering the Dead

RILEY CRUZ SERIES

Prequel Novella: Boneyard Thief

Book 1: Demon Relic Hunter

ACKNOWLEDGMENTS

Special thanks goes to my husband Chris, my fantastic editor Sara Lundberg, and to my amazing readers who love these characters as much as I do.

www.ingramcontent.com/pod-product-compliance
Lightning Source LLC
Chambersburg PA
CBHW061547210726
48287CB00006B/2106